14 DAYS--NOT RENEWABLE

Please Don't Lose the Date Card

THE
SCARLET
LETTERS

THE
SCARLET
LETTERS

LOUIS AUCHINCLOSS

Houghton Mifflin Company

BOSTON   NEW YORK

2003

Visit our Web site: www.houghtonmifflinbooks.com.

Library of Congress Cataloging-in-Publication Data

Auchincloss, Louis.
The scarlet letters / Louis Auchincloss.
p. cm.
ISBN 0-618-34159-5
1. Long Island (N.Y.) — Fiction. 2. Law firms — Fiction.
3. Adultery — Fiction. I. Title.

PS3501.U25S3 2003
813'.54—dc21   2003041726

Book design by Anne Chalmers
Typefaces: Janson Text, LH Didot, Arabesque Ornaments

Printed in the United States of America

MP 10 9 8 7 6 5 4 3 2 1

FOR MY GRANDDAUGHTER

HANNAH BONNER AUCHINCLOSS

THE
SCARLET
LETTERS

PROLOGUE

❧

In the midsummer of 1953 the coastal village of Glenville on the opulent north shore of Long Island was shaken by scandal. At least its principal citizens were so affected: summer and weekend residents, commuters to the big city and proprietors of the larger local businesses. It was not to be expected that the smaller folk would be much affected by adultery in the family of Ambrose Vollard, distinguished counsel though he was to many great corporations and the managing partner of the Wall Street law firm of Vollard, Kaye & Duer, known popularly as Vollard Kaye or simply Vollard K. But when the adulterer was none other than Rodman Jessup, not only the son-in-law and junior partner of Vollard but his special favorite and all-but-designated successor, a young man universally admired for his impeccable morals and high ideals, and when his partner in crime, Mrs. Lila Fisk, was a middle-aged Manhattan society woman of fading charms and loose behavior, the effect on the good burghers of Glenville was comparable to that of the Hebrews when Delilah cut off Samson's curly locks. A champion had inexplicably fallen; they could only raise their hands and deplore the degeneracy of the times. Small wonder that their planet was menaced with a third world war!

No one had seen a flaw in the Jessups' marriage. Lavinia, or

Vinnie, the most adored by Vollard of his three daughters, had introduced her future husband to her father when he was a law student at Columbia, almost as though she were bringing him the son he never had and was supposed to have passionately wanted. Pretty, bright, charming and amiable, now the mother of two daughters herself, Vinnie and her handsome husband were the undisputed leaders of Glenville's younger summer set.

Would Rod now come to his senses? Would he drop to his knees before this wronged bride and beg her forgiveness? Was not his legal career as well as his marriage at stake? But Rod showed no signs of repentance. He left his home in Glenville and his apartment in town and holed up in his club. He was seen at nightspots with the elegantly clad Mrs. Fisk. They posed for their picture together at a charity ball. Indeed, he seemed intent on flaunting the affair. Next it was heard that he had submitted his resignation to Vollard Kaye and that it had been accepted. Finally it became known that Vinnie was suing him for divorce in New York on the grounds of adultery, and that representing her in her father's firm was none other than Harry Hammersly, the young bachelor partner who had been known as Rod's best friend.

The ladies who gathered at noon on the terrace of the Glenville Beach Club to watch their children and grandchildren basking or playing on the sand below, or gazing out to sea at the white triangles of sailboats taking their positions for the afternoon race, were now even ordering an unusual second cocktail in their eagerness to prolong the fierce gossip over the scandal in the Vollard family. But a hush would fall on any group when their table was passed by a small plump lady in white with a shiny black hat and roving beady black eyes. It was Mrs. Ambrose Vollard herself, wife of the senior partner of the celebrated law firm and mother-in-law of the defecting adulterer, who radiated a mild and essentially unconcerned geniality on a community that admired her character and feared her tongue. She had sprung, as all Glenville knew and had always known, from the distant hub of Boston where she had been of the highest possible Brahmin caste, and always seemed tolerantly but perhaps the least bit condescendingly amused by the doings and sayings of people who claimed to be quite as much American as herself. She now greeted the table that she ultimately joined as cheerfully as if she didn't know exactly what they had been talking about, and was heard to reply to a brash and uninstructed new member of the club who actually had the effrontery to offer her sympathy on the recent scandal and asked if she had ever anticipated such a disaster. "Ah, my dear, any understanding of what has happened in my family would require a close knowledge of all the different personalities involved. You cannot expect a wife and mother, much less a mother-in-law, to be your guide in any such complexities." She turned now to survey the cove and the gathering boats. "They say young Tommy Taylor is favored to win the race today. What do you all think?"

But it was evident that they would rather think of the complexities to which she had glancingly referred.

1

IT WAS COMMONLY SAID, in the early 1900s, in the large and not undistinguished Manhattan social circle of the Vollard clan, of Ambrose, then a lad of twelve or thirteen, that he seemed the all-American boy: comely, tousle-haired, blue-eyed, grinning, the prototype of a youth out of Mark Twain or even Horatio Alger. But only a few years later he had grown into something quite different: a large, rather hulking type, almost menacingly muscular, whose good looks were darkened by an air of surly moodiness not quite redeemed by his brooding, now blue-gray eyes.

If there were, or at least had been, two Ambroses, it might have been because there seemed to be two Vollard families in which the boy had been reared. There was what might be called the older branch: Papa, Mama, son Russell, nicknamed "Stuffy" by his school pals, and daughter Elsie, known with unblushing sentimentality in the home as "Rosebud." And then there were the two younger children, the twins, Ambrose and fat little Bertha.

Why did that make two families? The answer, as in so many American social problems, must be sought in Mama. When Fanny Vollard had found herself the mother of two fine infants, the required son and the desired daughter, she supposed

4

that she had fulfilled her generative duties and could present a completed family to the proper ranks of her excellently proper relatives. But whether it was a too importunate husband — or one who lacked the discretion of Onan — she made the unwelcome discovery that she was again pregnant, and most uncomfortably so with twins, and was obliged to undergo a delivery that was not only excruciatingly painful but that almost cost her her life. Thereafter the partition that divided the two families was like the closed door of Fanny's bed chamber — shut, that is, to Papa, consigned to a back room of their Manhattan brownstone overlooking the bare yards, while his wife continued to occupy her comfortable and commodious apartment in the front of the house whose three large windows faced the street.

Taking up the Vollards in reverse order of their importance, Elias, Papa, was the first. He was a large, expensively clad gentleman with a big potbelly and features that might have been well enough in younger, leaner days, but which now bore the blankness of one who sought relief from real things in perfunctory tasks and compulsive habits. He looked the part of a sober and prosperous man of affairs, and indeed he sat on some important boards where his fixity of apparent attention concealed his daydreaming, but his ineptitude as an investor had reduced his wife's inherited capital far more than she knew, and he maintained only with difficulty their brownstone in town and the larger shingle cottage in Newport that she had taken over on her father's death and clung to with a tenacity that he dared not disturb. Elias's life consisted in forms; they were the only things of which he could be sure, and he clung to them as his salvation from an eternity of nothingness.

His son Russell, or "Stuffy," justified his nickname. He had a high brow, a large nose, a square chin and slickly combed, diminishing brown hair; his air of arrogant self-sufficiency was a wide shield to cover everything else. And "Rosebud" was a heavy, gushing, vaguely pretty blonde, subject to wild outbursts of fatuous enthusiasm, who once told her kid brother Ambrose that she would rather see him dead than a disbeliever in the divinity of Christ. What he replied disposed permanently of what little there was of her sibling affection.

This trio obviously needed a more robustly equipped individual to guide and manage them in the highways and byways of a New York and Newport life, and they had one in Mama. When one knew that Fanny Vollard had been born a de Peyster — she never mentioned it because she never had to — one knew not the most important thing about her but what she considered the most important. The de Peysters were old Knickerbocker stock, related to Van Rensselaers and Stuyvesants, and Fanny belonged to a minor branch of that tree which still looked askance at the new railroad and steel barons of the postbellum era, and disdained, unwisely, to seek marital alliances with Vanderbilts and Goulds. Remaining pure, she had married a "gentleman," and kept her eyes firmly fixed on the past, pronouncing "girl" "goyle" and "pearl" "poyle" in the aristocratic manner of the late eighteenth century, embarrassing her descendants who mistook it for a vulgar Brooklynese.

But Fanny had character. Diminutive, disciplined, with some hint of faded beauty, with lips virgin to rouge and cheeks to powder and hair unwaved by machinery, she possessed a dignity and quiet force that was almost regal. Few suspected that her air and demeanor constituted a fort to protect a garrison of inner fears, fear of contagious diseases, unprincipled men, stock market upsets and, above all, a day of judgment waiting at the end of the road and the very real possibility of hellfire. What bore her up was her pride and her ability — or was it an instinct — to draft other humans into a regiment to afford her both moral and material support.

If it was an instinct it was that of a parasite plant or animal. Fanny would reach out, presumably unconsciously, to grasp in a tight ineluctable embrace the neighboring organism most endowed to supply her own deficiencies. In Elias she sensed the male who would always sympathize with her valetudinarianism, surround her with the comforts she imagined she required, and admire the fortitude with which she bore her anxieties and depressions. In her son Stuffy she flared the insecurity behind his pomposity and in her daughter Rosebud the anxiety beneath her little spring showers of good will, and knew that a mother's love and approval, or at least the easily adopted appearance of such, would be rewarded by a devotion gratifyingly servile.

Fanny's instinct may even have been what guided her steps as far as Philadelphia where she consulted the famous Dr. S. Weir Mitchell, whose popular prescribed "rest cure" for wealthy society ladies totally justified to the eyes of Elias and the two elder children the long hours that Fanny spent in her chaise longue and the hushed atmosphere of a household where family and servants silently and uncomplainingly performed what otherwise might have been considered her duties.

But all that left out the twins. Indeed it did. The parasite at once recognizes the organism that will not welcome its octuple embrace. Fanny felt in the very agony of her delivery that Ambrose and Bertha would not be her subjects, at least not willingly. The remedy for this was simple enough: it was to make it appear to the world that the twins, rowdy and ungovernable juniors, had by their own stubborn and ungrateful natures rejected the love that their irreproachable mother so freely offered them. Few guests at the family board could have detected any reprehensible difference between the ways Fanny treated her elder and younger offspring. But perhaps a keen one might have.

"Ambrose, my dear, don't wolf your food down that way, and do, child, try to sit up a little straighter. The way Russell does. Of course, I realize that Russell is older and has had the advantage of boarding school discipline, but you can still take him as an example. There, dear, that's better. And Bertha, darling, how many times must I tell you that ladies don't put their elbows on the table? You don't see Rosebud doing that, do you? Oh, but I must stop calling Elsie by that name, now she's almost a debutante, mustn't I? And Bertha, dear, remember that we want you too to be a debutante one day, and debutantes certainly never put their elbows on the table."

"But I don't want to be a debutante! Ever!"

Bertha's retort demonstrated the difference between her reaction to the maternal solicitude and that of her twin. Bertha, a large, rather blocky girl with a very square chin and wide scornful brown eyes was not taken in for a moment. Ambrose was. He did not feel any engulfing warmth towards a mother whose frail health protected her from his bear hugs, but he tended to assume that she was essentially like other mothers. And so he continued to suppose until, at fourteen, he was sent off to boarding school.

Chelton, an Episcopal church academy for boys a few miles north of Boston, boasted a handsome campus of red-bricked, white-columned buildings around a well-kept oval green lawn at one end of which stood a gray Gothic chapel. Ambrose, now a husky athletic youth with friendly manners, was immediately popular, his only drawback being a hot temper and quick and effective use of his fists. Such fits were followed by moods of sullen silence that his pals charitably attributed to remorse. His high grades and skill at football won him the approval of both the boys and the faculty, and in his next to last year he was considered a candidate in the following autumn for the high honor of senior prefect. But it was not to be.

He had become uncomfortably aware that he was never in a position to return the hospitality of his friends, whose visiting parents often asked him to supper on Saturday nights at the local inn where they spent the weekend. For his parents never visited the school. Indeed, they were almost the only parents who didn't.

At home on Christmas vacation Ambrose finally complained about this to the always sympathetic Bertha. "They used to come up when Stuffy was in school," he pointed out ruefully.

"Ah, but that was Stuffy!" Bertha exclaimed, with heavy sarcasm. "You're not comparing yourself to the great Stuffy, are you? Pardon *you*, if you do!"

"Papa says Mama's health isn't up to the long trip to school," Ambrose insisted, irritated now by her tone.

"Isn't up to four hours in a comfortable parlor car! Well, it was certainly up to it when Stuffy was at Chelton. And she was just as set on her daffy 'rest cure' then as she is now. Has she ever praised you for standing second in your form? Has she even mentioned the fact that you may be in line to be senior prefect?"

"She did say something about it."

"When you called it to her attention."

"It's true I did tell her about it," he admitted reluctantly.

"And she already knew because I had bragged about it to her!" Bertha cried in triumph. "She knew but didn't say a word! And when Stuffy, who had rock bottom grades, was finally made rober to the rector in chapel, to keep his page in the yearbook from being a total blank, didn't she and Papa pop the champagne corks? And when Rosebud got B for effort in her gym class, didn't they practically declare a holiday?"

"You're so bitter about Mama, Bertha."

"Bitter? That's not the word. I hate her! And so would you if you weren't as blind as a bat. Or blind as a boy, I should say!"

This brief but illuminating interchange marked the beginning of a profound alteration in Ambrose's personality and general outlook on life. Thus far he had tended to denigrate his twin with the condescension of a male teenager, regarding her as a somewhat silly and vastly opinionated girl who was always pushing her unthinking self into the councils of her betters, but he began to perceive that she was able to make brutally clear all kinds of things of which he had previously been only dimly aware. Now when he moved close to his mother to give her the customary morning or evening kiss, and she placed a mildly restraining hand on his shoulder it was distaste, and not, as he had previously imagined, to guard her frail body from the possibly unpremeditated assault of a wild and undependable beast. And then, alerted by jealousy, he took careful note when she put her arms around Stuffy's neck or chucked Rosebud under the chin.

Oh yes, it had become a different world. Seventeen is a violent age, and it doesn't take much to turn the landscape sour. When Ambrose went fishing with his father now, in the latter's fly club in the Catskills, he would no longer, on a wide rock by an idling stream at noon, while they ate their sandwiches and drank their beer, relate to him his tales of school and football. He knew now that his parent never listened; Elias Vollard was perfectly content with the sunshine and silence and nothingness.

If the rock basis of parentage is once displaced the rest of the edifice will soon cave in. The cloud that darkened the home soon caught the school in its shadow. Wasn't it part and parcel of the same fabric? Surely the deity so punctiliously worshiped by his starchly dressed parents on Sunday, so regularly invoked at grace before meals and so grovelingly implored at night, was the same who presided over the Chelton chapel and inspired the headmaster's throaty sermons about boys keeping themselves pure for the pure maidens they might one day hope to wed. Dr. Close himself, a small plump man with toadlike features, and as Ambrose now saw him, a Trollopian snob, conducted a fifth-form class in sacred studies in which the sharp note of his once docile student's emancipation was first heard.

The class discussion was of the superiority of monotheism, as devised by Jews, Moslems and, best of all, Christians, to the worship of a more populated Olympus by pagan rites.

"But why, sir?" Ambrose wanted to know. "Might it not be better to have several gods rather than just one? Is there anyone of our faith wiser than Socrates? Or Cicero? Or even Augustus Caesar?"

"But from the very multitude of pagan deities, Vollard, must one not infer that they have different personalities? Different qualities? If they were all the same, they would have to be one, would they not? And if they are different they cannot all be perfect; only one can be that. Which means that all but one would be imperfect. And imperfection implies faults. Why should we worship a god with faults? One, for example, who would turn a maiden into a tree for resisting his lust?"

The headmaster nodded to the class as if to invite the titters that respectfully followed, and turned back to his notes as if he had coped with Ambrose's interruption. But he hadn't.

"But it seems to me, sir, that this one God had faults."

"How do you mean, Vollard?" The tone was graver now. "And be careful in how you state it. You mustn't tread lightly on the faith of others."

"I can only say what I think, sir. Is a god perfect — is he even very good — if he created organisms that could only survive by eating each other?"

Dr. Close frowned. But he wished to keep at least the appearance of a free discussion alive. "There are things that pass our understanding, Vollard. Their meaning may not be divulged in this lifetime."

"But this God, sir, not only created men who had to kill to live. He wants them to praise him and magnify him forever! If a man did that, wouldn't we call him a pompous ass?"

"That will be all, Vollard. We have heard enough from you. More than enough. I'll see you after class. And now let me hear from some of the rest of you."

A much less adventuresome discussion followed this.

Somewhat to Ambrose's surprise, but not at all to the alleviation of his new doubts, the headmaster, normally so high and distant with the boys, accorded him two long individual sessions in which he mildly and tediously lectured him on Christian orthodoxy. He had, after all, a soul to save. But Ambrose was obdurate. He stoutly declined to consider being confirmed in the church and refused even to soft-pedal his efforts to spread his atheism among his classmates.

This resulted not in his being expelled, but in his being sent home for a term.

"I am running a church school, Vollard," the headmaster explained, with a sad but dismissing shake of his head. "And I cannot tolerate the presence here of an active proselytizer of what we used to call heresy. It is my hope and belief that when our boys have graduated and are turned out in the world, their faith will be strong enough to withstand arguments such as yours. But while they are young and impressionable I deem it my duty to protect them from confusing elements. If after you have talked to your parents and reflected on my words, and have taken a more enlightened attitude towards our faith, you will be welcome back at school."

"You needn't worry, sir. I won't bother you again. I'll never come back here."

The headmaster sighed but made no answer, and Ambrose was sent home that very day. He was given no further opportunity to corrupt his classmates.

At home his suspension caused less of a scene than he had expected. His parents seemed put out but hardly surprised. His father confined himself to a few gruff and reproving remarks, and it was quickly arranged that he should be enrolled in a private day school — the new popularity of boarding institutions with affluent parents who dreaded the effect of city streets on their boys had depleted the ranks of the old urban academies and caused them to welcome even heretical recruits. Fanny Vollard, however, had a few matters to settle with her disappointing younger son, and she subjected him to a quiet lecture in her boudoir.

"I don't understand you, Ambrose. And I don't think I ever really have. You and Bertha have never shown me half the love and affection that Russell and Rosebud have. Perhaps I don't deserve it. Who knows? But I am your mother, and it will always be my duty, however painful, to point out to you any wrong road you are taking. I have, of course, read carefully your headmaster's report. I see that you have prided yourself as a free thinker among the benighted, in which class I am sure you include your parents as well as the faculty of Chelton School. You think you are brave and bold and forward thinking. But in fact you are just another impudent boy determined to bring down anyone or anything that threatens to be higher or bigger than yourself. If you fail you will look a fool, and if you succeed — which God forbid — you will simply find yourself pinned in the wreckage."

The terrible thing about Fanny was that she never thought of children as children. The moment they offended her they were just as much adults as herself, and she struck back with every arrow in her quiver. Mortals were divided into her friends and her enemies, and once she had spotted a child as among the latter, she had no more mercy on him than for a pickpocket in the street.

Ambrose trembled a bit at the impact of her hostility, but he soon rallied his inner forces. He was learning that if he was to lead his life without any significant parental love, he might also dispose with worrying unduly about parental opposition. He never bothered to explain his rejection of orthodoxy to his mother — indeed he hardly bothered to explain it to himself; he knew that her mind was closed to argument, and for the next year, until he entered Columbia College, he lived with his parents in a kind of armed truce. This was not difficult with two persons as self-absorbed as Elias and Fanny, particularly as the routine of their domestic life was as fixed as the rotation of the planets. He had only to avoid any open friction, which, with a father who at home passed the greater part of his time alone in his study, the silence of which was broken only by the occasional clink of decanters, and with a mother intent upon preserving her body from the least exhaustion, was no great task. And his mornings were all spent in class and his afternoons in the school gym.

It helped, too, that Stuffy and Rosebud were both now married and away from home. Ambrose's family life, and even social life, were mostly reduced to Bertha, on whom her mother had largely given up after her adamant refusal to "come out" or even to attend any debutante parties. Bertha, stout, plain and emphatic, was allowed to come and go pretty much as she pleased. She adored Ambrose, and her passionate espousal of his side in any family dispute contributed to the comparative silence in which meals at the Vollards were held. And when, in Ambrose's first year at Columbia, he came home drunk one night and encountered his shocked mother in a corridor, it was Bertha who quieted the ensuing furor by suggesting that he move to a college dormitory, which the very next day he did.

He had chosen Columbia because he had no wish to resume his old acquaintance with Chelton classmates at Yale or Harvard. The Chelton values, which he now associated with the parental ones, he had repudiated. As an angry young man he cultivated the radical elements of his new institution, inveighed against the trusts and found President Taft a sad step backwards after the great Teddy. But his political liberalism was tempered by moods of deep depression when nothing seemed really worth fighting for, when the world seemed a flourishing garden only for such noodles as Stuffy and Rosebud, and a desert for the likes of him. Then he would turn away from his dogmatic and obstreperous new friends and solace himself alone in his room with whiskey. He had no opportunity to travel or even to wine and dine expensively; his father, fearful that he would give his money to some leftist cause, kept him on a spare allowance.

But he had one salvation; he read. As with his hero, Teddy Roosevelt, reading with him was a "disease." He reveled in the English poets, especially Byron and Shelley, whose fire and cynicism he tried to emulate; he delighted in the madness of Dostoyevsky, the oratory of Milton's Satan, and the violence of Ahab in the newly appreciated *Moby-Dick*. He wrote stories himself, about evil men who preyed on dolts, women who betrayed their lovers, bankers who degenerated into vampires, and clergymen who dwindled into sheep. He sent them to magazine editors who invariably rejected them, though one more percipient reader commented on the vigor of his style and suggested that he try his hand at more neutral subject matter. "For neutral read neuter," he snorted in disgust.

It was Bertha who promoted the idea of his going to law school. She was just as antagonistic to the old world as he was, but more objective. And she was less wrapped up in Bertha than he was in Ambrose. She was capable of putting herself in his shoes while preserving her own outlook. But then she loved him, and he, as yet, loved no one.

"Male and female twins aren't really twins, you know," she told him one day as they lunched in a Broadway café, which they frequently did now that she was enrolled in Barnard. "Obviously they can't resemble each other in all respects. *Vive la différence!* as the French say, though I'm not sure what good it's done *me*. But the point is that you've got a bigger brain than I do. And a bigger spirit, a bigger future. Your trouble is that you don't know what to do with it. You need time to decide. And the classic way to spend that time is in law school. For whatever you ultimately decide on, a law degree will be a bonus. Except perhaps in medicine, but I don't see you becoming a doctor."

Of course he had thought of this. But now she helped it to take root. "Will Papa stake me to it?" he wondered.

"Leave that to me!"

In fact she had already crossed that bridge, by persuading her parents that the study of law was really the study of law and order and might have a mollifying effect on their wide-eyed son.

Which it did. Or rather which Professor Gideon Gregg did. He was a small dry neat bald sexagenarian, with a voice so low that he lectured through an amplifier, who had devoted his life to the study and teaching of contract law, with rare but well-paid appearances in court as an expert witness to edify the bench. He was supposed to have thus answered a judge's question as to who was the foremost authority in his field: "I believe, your honor, that Mr. Williston at Harvard is generally deemed the second." Unlike many law professors he disdained the barking approach; he was invariably kind and courteous to his students, and was notorious, when questioning one of them in class, for offering broad hints as to the correct answer. He wanted to believe that every man or woman seated before him was a natural lawyer, but he nonetheless had a keen eye for a real talent, and when he found a paper of Ambrose's on unilateral contracts unusually perspicacious, he called him into his office and offered him on the spot a job assisting him in revising an edition of his famous casebook. It was, of course, quite a load to take on in addition to Ambrose's class work, but as the stipend was generous, thanks to Gregg's soft heart, and as the Vollard allowance, from a still doubting father, was still on the stingy side, he jumped at the chance.

The close relationship that ensued between master and apprentice gave Ambrose his first real purpose and incentive in life. He came to see his wonderful little mentor as an inspired artist who could use words as his tools to clamp the golden wires of civility around the dark chaos of life. Offer and acceptance, good faith and bad, the meeting or non-meeting of minds, consideration and specific performance, breach and damages — the areas of contractual obligation opened up to him like a massive clearing in a dense dark threatening jungle, and the beauty of Gideon Gregg's prose in the essay portions of his casebook, the tight flashing mesh of his Anglo-Saxon short words and his Latinized long ones, seamlessly concise

17

and pregnant with meaning, provided Ambrose with a kind of creed, or art, or even faith that might be almost enough to live on.

By the middle of his second year at law school Ambrose had completed his work on the casebook, which was just as well, as he had accepted, at the professor's strong urging, an editorship on the Law Journal that would henceforth preempt his every spare moment.

"Whatever else happens to me in life, sir," he told his mentor, "I know now that I will always be a lawyer."

Gregg stared at him in astonishment. "Great Scott, my boy, was there ever a doubt in your mind about that? What the devil else did you come to law school for?"

"Oh, I heard it was a good preparation for almost everything."

"It's a good preparation for the practice of law, that's what it is. And if ever I saw a born attorney, it's you, my boy. If you do anything else, you're a fool, and if you're that it's time I retired. For if I'm wrong on that, I'm wrong on everything."

"But is it necessary to practice, sir? Couldn't I be a teacher like you and the writer of treatises?"

Gregg was silent for a moment, and his face expressed the seriousness of his thought. "You could, yes. But I think your particular forte will be for an active practice. I see you as a fighter, my boy. Nor do I for a minute minimize that. The judge, the law professor, the treatise writer and the practicing lawyer are all equally indispensable to our sacred profession. The law comes out of our words: words penned for books and treatises in sober reflection, words used less temperately in briefs and oral argument, words chosen wisely in opinions or dramatically in classrooms, it's all the same game!"

Ambrose had another talk with the professor about his future a year later, in the spring before his graduation.

"Am I not correct, Ambrose, in supposing that Charles de Peyster is a relative of yours?"

"He's my uncle, sir. My mother's brother."

"May I suggest, then, that you apply to his firm for a position? It's one of the first, perhaps the best, of the great corporation law firms of our city. I have had the occasion to testify for them in a number of cases. They do fine work."

"But I'm afraid, sir, I've been rather remiss in my family duties. I have seen my uncle only at Christmas or birthday gatherings. And I'm afraid he may have formed an unfavorable opinion of me when I dropped out of Chelton."

"Pish tush, that water's long under the bridge. You'll find he'll take a very different view of you when he hears *my* recommendation. And that he is certainly going to have!"

2

UNCLE CHARLEY HAD MANY of the de Peyster characteristics: he was grave of demeanor, deeply conservative in his attitudes — domestic, political and economic — darkly and faultlessly dressed, dignified in bearing, measured of speech. But he differed drastically from his sister Fanny in that he cut a figure of considerable importance in the social and business worlds and cared about cutting such a figure. For all his disdain of an increasingly multiracial and multicultural New York and what he considered its vulgar innovations, for all his reluctance to associate with Irish Catholics or Jews, he studied the changes in his world with care and caution and learned precisely what compromises were required for a successful navigator of such turbulent water and just when hoisting the de Peyster flag could be a signal of triumph and when dipping it could be a judicious surrender. His mind and legal abilities, though keen enough, were not of the high caliber to have brought him by themselves to eminence at the bar, but when added to his impressive appearance, his high social connections and his smooth assurance of attracting major clients, the combination carried him to the senior partnership in Dallas, Kaye & de Peyster that he had never doubted would one day be his. Majestic but gracious, he inspired in the roughest of rough diamonds among the firm's large and variegated clientele something like the awe which a Spanish conquistador might have instilled in a native Aztec or Inca.

He understood at once the value of Professor Gregg's recommendation of his nephew; it confirmed an unspoken suspicion on his part that his sister was too self-centered to have any true comprehension of an even mildly rebellious child. He had heard her complaints about Ambrose's "atheism" with the same cool but neutral silence of a Medici cardinal hearing of the indictment of a Galileo. He would only interfere when it paid him to interfere, and this happened when he hired Ambrose on his own account, the other available openings in his firm having been filled by graduates of Harvard Law School, the institution then almost exclusively favored by his partners. Years later this decision, like most that Charles de Peyster made, redounded to his own benefit, for when he aged and began to fail, it was his rising relative who went to bat for him and saved his unduly swollen percentage of profits earned by younger men from being reduced by a hungry partnership.

At first under his uncle's guidance but rapidly on his own merits Ambrose's rise in the firm was steady and seemingly ineluctable. He not only loved his work, he devoured it, putting in hours that surprised even the most industrious of an already industrious organization. He attacked the thorniest of great corporation problems with a kind of fierce delight, and in his admiration of power and his excitement at implementing it he lost almost every tinge of his youthful economic liberalism. He turned his reforming energy instead to studying the composition and administration of the firm that was to be the tool of his creative thinking and made plans in his head for its better development if he should ever find himself in charge. He would concentrate, for example, on improving its esprit de corps. No lawyer would ever be hired either as a partner or clerk collaterally: every ultimate member of the firm would start as an associate right out of law school, secure in the knowledge that his only rivals for partnership would be the men starting with him. Any associate passed over for partnership, a majority of which if the firm was to be kept a manageable size, would be assured of an equally well or even better paid job in a client or sister firm. Profits would be divided evenly among the partners, with certain gradations upwards with age and downwards with old age. The energy and unity of the firm as a team would not be dissipated by foreign branches; there would be one office and one alone. Oh, he had it all worked out!

As he rose in the firm Ambrose was careful to cultivate close friendships with his fellow clerks, particularly those in whom he saw the most brilliant legal future. He discarded the somewhat shaggy appearance he had adopted in academe, and took care now to be well groomed, with his thick, prematurely graying hair properly clipped and combed, his square chin held up but not arrogantly, his large lanky figure no longer slouching but straight. People meeting Ambrose knew that they were in contact with a man who knew what he was doing and what he could do for them.

His family now came round to something like an appreciation. His father gave him money that he no longer needed, and his mother allowed him to kiss her without placing a hand on his shoulder.

Bertha was delighted with him, but not surprised; she was only disappointed that his work prevented him from having a social life as animated as his legal one. Stuffy actually brought him some slight and undesirable business, and Rosebud, who despite a rich husband had only a small property of her own, named him an executor of her will.

There were still periods when his old black moods would descend upon him, days, though infrequent, when he would without excuse fail to appear at the office and drink inordinately in his small apartment, and growl at his new image in the mirror and confound himself for succumbing to the false standards of the old world of the de Peysters and falser ones of the new world of the Goulds and Fisks. Yet he was still beginning to wonder if, given the powers of a president with a majority behind him in both houses of Congress, he would do more than add a few teeth to the Sherman Act and lower the tariffs. The world, as Justice Holmes had said, wouldn't be much better off if the riches of the rich were scattered among the innumerable poor. It would be Ambrose's function, if he had any at all, to grease the wheels of such financial machinery as kept things going. But his law firm, if it ever should be his, would at least be a beacon of honesty! Uncle Charley was all very well, but he had his moments of compromise with men who emitted a faint scent of brimstone. Ambrose would have to wait. But he could wait! Then he would put the bottle down, take a shower and go back to work.

There was little time for love in his busy life, but there was some. When his uncle, foreseeing the day when his nephew might become a partner and desiring him to have experience in all the firm's departments, transferred him for a season into the field of trusts and estates, Ambrose found himself spending more time than was actually required drawing a will and trusts for the pretty and flirtatious young bride of an aging financier. Uncle Charley, who had a sharp nose for the ultra-proper, scented trouble early, and, anxious not to have the financier upset, summoned his nephew for a little "chat." To forestall resentment he cloaked his caution in terms of general advice.

"You never knew my partner, Oscar Tully, did you, Ambrose? He retired before you joined us. He was not quite a man of our background — he had had to make his own way in life — but he was a first-class lawyer, and he had a wise and pithy way of expressing basic truths. 'Give a lady client everything you have above the waist, nothing from below.'"

Ambrose was amused by his own shock at so unexpected a crudity. "You mean never have an affair with a client, sir? Do you imply that I'm in danger of one?"

"No, no, dear boy, I'm merely stating a principle. Though of course you're a handsome enough young fellow. And unattached, too. There are uncles who might say, If the shoe fits, wear it."

"It seems to me you just have."

"Well, there's no harm done, in any case. But that isn't the real matter I have to discuss with you today. I want you to go to Boston and do a little job for me. I say a little job, though it may take three or four weeks. You've heard of the Reverend Philemon Shattuck up there?"

"The great preacher? Yes, of course."

"He's not only a great preacher and an old Harvard classmate of mine, but, like many Massachusetts divines, he's a gentleman of considerable wealth. There's a rather messy and nasty accounting proceeding going on there involving the estate of a bachelor brother of his, a mistress claiming this and that, and so forth. He doesn't want to get too much involved in it, though of course he and his sisters have to put in appearances, but he wants a smart lawyer to keep an eye on what's going on and check on the family counsel, in whom he has limited confidence. That's where you come in. I know you haven't been admitted up there, but you can attend the hearings as his private watchdog and tell him if you think it's advisable to send in additional troops."

"But won't the family counsel object?"

"They needn't even know about it. And if they do find out, so what? Nobody's going to pick a row with Dr. Shattuck. You'll be staying with him and his family. It's a mansion on Commonwealth Avenue, and I've no doubt you'll find yourself very comfortable. Besides, there are five unmarried daughters, all reasonably attractive."

"Do you suggest I might have my pick of them?"

"I shouldn't be surprised. A strapping New York attorney could be a rather tempting morsel to a closely guarded Boston debutante. Of course, there are a couple of brothers, and a seven-way division can wreak havoc on a family fortune, but plenty of those saving Bostonians are even richer than generally supposed."

"Do I strike you as so mercenary, sir?"

"You don't strike me as anything, silly boy. Can't you see I'm talking in generalities?"

"But if the shoe fits . . . ?"

"Exactly! Then wear it!"

"Have you any advice as to which daughter I should start on?"

"You'll want me to propose for you next!" Uncle Charley retorted with a gruff laugh. "But seriously, Ambrose, and coming down to individualities, it's time you thought of settling down. I've always said that an associate is less valuable to us both in the year that he's courting and in the one following his marriage, so let's get that period behind us as soon as we can. For I don't have to tell such a smart aleck as you that you have a future in this firm!"

Ambrose smiled to himself at the idea obviously in his uncle's mind that he had to be got away from the pretty client before she jeopardized his career, but he knew it would do him no harm to be considered something of a philanderer provided he did not carry it too far. He lightheartedly adapted himself to his new role and journeyed north to visit the Shattucks.

The house was as impressively strong as its famous architect, Henry H. Richardson, could make it; its stout red brick appearance and heavy Romanesque arches suggested that the zealous faith which it enshrined was ready to be militantly defended against any heresies that managed to flourish, even in the frosty New England air. The Reverend Philemon Shattuck, a hearty man of God, made Ambrose robustly welcome in a female household ruled but by no means cowed by its ebullient head, and he found himself almost at once congenial with the middle one of the five daughters. Harriet, or "Hetty," was a pert, pale-faced and somewhat diminutive young lady, with unwaved auburn hair and darting, shrewdly observing black eyes, not indeed particularly pretty but alive, alert and voluble. He also noted the perfect family unity and good will: the other four, having noted her immediate interest in the newcomer and his seemingly equal response, at once left the field to her. Boston was certainly not like New York.

On the first Sunday of his visit he went with the family to divine services and to hear Dr. Shattuck preach in that other, even more awesome structure of Mr. Richardson's, Trinity Church, whose vast auditorium was filled to capacity. Ambrose listened, impressed but unpersuaded, to the sometimes mellifluous, sometimes thundering oration of the great cleric. His theme was happiness, the glorious happiness that should attend a true faith, even in the midst of grievous tribulations, a faith mighty enough to have inspired early Christian martyrs to sing joyful anthems at the very moment that famished lions approached them in the arena. Ambrose could not but marvel that so much polished and splendid oratory should be expended on so fatuous a theme.

It was a beautiful day of early spring, and he suggested to Hetty, who had sat beside him in the family pew, that they walk back to the house. Crossing the square he paused to look back at the bold and rugged magnificence of the somber temple they had just quit.

"It's really, isn't it, to our century, at least up here in Boston, what Chartres was to France in the thirteenth? It expresses the hardy faith of the pilgrim fathers."

"Not quite," she cautioned him. "Aren't you forgetting it's an Episcopal house of worship, a limb, if you like, of the Church of England, and that's precisely what they came over here to get away from?"

"I guess what the British can't conquer they reconquer."

She turned to walk on. "At least in Boston whatever a church stands for, we let it stand clear. We don't bury it under skyscrapers, the way you do in New York."

"Not yet," he said grimly.

"You mean we'll come to it? I suppose we must. New York, like Britain, can be counted on to win in the end."

"Omnia vincit vulgarity!"

"That's what Mr. Henry James seems to think. Have you read his *American Scene*?"

"No. I find life too short for his late style." He spoke sincerely. He was no Jacobite, but it impressed him that she was.

"That's your loss. He cites the example of Trinity Church on lower Broadway being dwarfed by its colossal neighbor, an office building erected by its very trustees!"

"You see that as a symbol of our era? That business dominates the cross? That business *is* the cross?"

"I'm not so keen on drawing conclusions, Mr. Vollard. But I like to face facts."

"For what purpose? For your own diversion?"

"Isn't that enough? Facts are really all we have to go on. But we have to be sure first that they *are* facts. Trinity Church is put out of face by an adjacent skyscraper. That seems plain enough. It gives me something to start with."

"But the very way you state it leads inevitably to a hostile conclusion. You're a cynic, Miss Shattuck, though you may try to conceal it."

"The way you conceal what you think about my father?"

"How do you know what I think of your father?"

"By the way your eyes roamed around our dining room the first night you stayed with us. You were thinking, Isn't this pretty posh for a man of the cloth? Is it the Gospel according to Saint Matthew or *Barchester Towers*?"

"Miss Shattuck, I'm beginning to be afraid of you."

"You mean because I spied a fact?"

"More because I dread the conclusion."

"And what would that be?"

"That I'm an ungrateful and ungracious guest."

"But I've come to no such conclusion! As to gratitude I see no call for it — you've come here to help us — and as to manners, yours have been above reproach."

"And manners are what count?"

"Well, certainly as much as unuttered thoughts, over which we have no power."

"Then I needn't be afraid of you?"

"I don't think you need be in the least afraid of me, Mr. Vollard."

They were soon on first-name terms, and in the ensuing fortnight became good friends indeed. His duties in following the Shattuck case consisted largely in attending the court sessions; his evenings were free to dine with the Shattucks or take Hetty and one of her sisters to a concert or play. And sometimes they would sit apart from the others in a corner of the long dark-paneled parlor, glinting with old silver pieces, and talk. Nobody interrupted them. He was marked as Hetty's beau.

Perhaps it was a bit premature. He found her provocative but reserved, challenging in her inquiries but moderate in her tone, tending to be at once sarcastic and commonsensical. She never said or did anything that would be classified as flirting, yet he was convinced that he had made a definite dent in her affections. Had he wanted to? He wasn't sure. He certainly hadn't wanted not to. Still, there was no question in his mind that she was the very opposite of the florid type of beauty that had thus far stirred his senses. He had no particular hankering to sleep with her, but he was sufficiently aware of the cruder side of his nature — as revealed in sundry episodes — to know that he was quite capable of mating with any passably attractive female.

One evening he amused himself by probing into the question of her attitude towards her famous father and his hearty evangelicalism. He scented dissent behind the bland wall of her apparently total loyalty.

"I can't help wondering what sort of a Christian you are, Hetty. You're certainly not strictly orthodox. I mean you don't strike me as one who swallows the story of Jonah's being swallowed by the whale."

"Can't there be different ways of interpreting scripture?"

"You mean you can twist it to mean anything you please?"

"No. To mean what a serious and impartial mind can deduce."

"And that will be God's truth?"

"One hopes it will be truth."

"You're elusive, Hetty. I can never pin you down."

"Why should you want to?"

"Oh, to know where I stand with you, I suppose. Or even if I want to stand with you. I don't really think I'm a Christian at all. I certainly don't have any truck with the idea that Jesus was divine. I guess I fit into the school that holds he was a simple and rather harmless fanatic about whom a monstrous legend was created by a clever priesthood. My family's religious attitude has always struck me as the quintessence of hollow gentility."

Hetty smiled. She was not in the least shocked. "In Boston we might call you a transcendentalist."

"That would clean me up, would it?"

"Well, enough so we could ask you to dinner. Or at least to come in afterwards."

He was suddenly almost angry. "Can you never take anything seriously?"

Her face became blank at this. "Oh, I'm serious enough. Isn't it you who are being rather reckless? Isn't it you who's rocking the boat?"

"Don't boats sometimes need rocking?"

"It's better to wait till we're a little closer to shore."

"You'd die, wouldn't you, Hetty, to maintain the status quo? To keep intact the little world that meekly worships your father and his God?"

Something almost like a frown for a moment clouded her brow. "My father does no harm to anyone. And he makes hundreds of people happier than they otherwise might be."

"By stuffing their heads with fairy tales!" Of course, he knew that he had gone too far. He didn't care. The unruffled pallor of her attention stifled him.

"What would you offer them instead?" was her cool inquiry.

"Oh, maybe something that you just called truth."

"I can only respond with Pilate's question."

At this he threw what last discretion he had to the winds. The others had already retired for the night, and they were now alone in the parlor, having assured Dr. Shattuck that they would turn off the lights. Ambrose had even started to do so, and the increased darkness suited his blackening mood. He turned back to her.

"You have no concept of what sort of man I am!" he exclaimed. "You'd despise me if you did!"

"Don't be too sure of that."

"How would you feel if I told you that one of your attractions to me was your money?"

She had remained quietly seated while he busied himself about the room. "I should probably wonder if you'd find it enough. I daresay you've heard greatly exaggerated amounts. Pa says people always think one is poorer or richer than one is."

He gaped. "You wouldn't *mind* being married for your money?"

"I certainly would if that were my suitor's only consideration. But if it were merely another item in the inventory of my charms, I would have to accept it in almost any man who wanted to marry me. At least here in Boston. And from what I've heard about New York, it's not a city devoid of material concerns. Even a millionaire might covet my dowry. He might see it as a guarantee that *he* wasn't being married for his money."

"You are certainly a very practical woman," he muttered.

"But that doesn't mean that I wouldn't want virtues to balance the material factor. As Macduff says of Malcolm's asserted vices: 'All these are portable, with other graces weighed.'"

Ambrose picked up the quotation with a fierce delight. "'But I have none!'" he cried. "'Nay, had I power I should pour the sweet milk of concord into hell, uproar the universal peace, confound all unity on earth!'"

"Well, we're both Shakespeare lovers anyway," she said, rising to help him turn off the last lamps. "And that in itself might be almost enough. But I warn you, Ambrose. If you think you can turn me off with the list of your imagined faults, I'm not taken in. Like Hamlet, I know a hawk from a handsaw."

The next days were deeply troubling ones for Ambrose. It was perfectly clear now that Hetty was ready to receive and willing to accept his proposal of marriage, that she had carefully weighed him in a mind not liable to deception and had come to the conclusion that he was worthy of the strong affection he had aroused. It was also clear to him that she did not regard him as in any way obligated to make such a proposal and that she deemed his conduct, far from seductive, to have been strictly that of a gentleman, a guest in her father's house and an agreeable friend. If he chose to leave their relationship at that, there would be no recriminations, no tears or fuss, no unseemly expressions of disappointment. The little woman was a lady, and a great lady at that.

A signal point in her favor was that she would require no false or hypocritical avowals of eternal passion. She would take him just as he was, a man who wanted a wife because a wife and children were what every sensible male should want, and a wife whose grace, decorum, social position and, yes, even money would smooth his progress to the success to which he naturally aspired and which he certainly deserved. To the world she would be the perfect spouse, and in private the perfect mate for a man of his doubts, depressions and soaring ambition. And he for her? Well, wasn't that *her* lookout? And wasn't she admirably equipped to look out for herself? Was knowing that love was more on one side than the other really taking advantage of her? Wasn't it almost always the case?

SOMEWHAT TO HIS SURPRISE Hetty went along with her parents' desire for a large wedding reception in their big shingle beach house in Nahant. Some three hundred of Boston's best gathered in the big tent erected on the lawn; it was a dressy and festive occasion. Ambrose's parents were delighted with the whole affair; they certainly thought that their younger son had done a great deal better than anyone could have expected from his youth. And Ambrose finally decided that they were right.

3

When a young man is furnished with the right job to fit
his talents and ambition and the right wife for his social and
domestic needs, his advance in the world, barring the absence
of Lady Luck, should be smooth and steady, and such was the
case with Ambrose. Even America's entry into the war in 1917
favored him, for as an army first lieutenant he was not sent to
the trenches, as he had requested, but assigned instead to the
war secretary's office in Washington, where his business experience enabled him to serve importantly in the field of arms
production and brought him in close touch with several mag-
nates who were later to join the swelling ranks of his clients.

Even the Grim Reaper proved his ally. The year 1923
marked the death of Uncle Charley, followed quickly by that of
two other senior partners, and in the sudden void of the firm
leadership Ambrose, still in his thirties, found himself cata-
pulted into its head management. Nothing could stop him
now. He was able at last to implement all his plans for the organization of a "perfect" law firm, and in the due course of time
the newly named Vollard, Kaye & Duer came to be deemed by
many the first in Wall Street for its expertise, its industry, its
interior discipline and high esprit de corps. And Ambrose's
fame, as he moved comfortably into his fifth decade, not only

as the wisest and shrewdest of counselors but as a witty and hearty companion, made him everywhere in demand as a speaker, a toastmaster, a cornerstone layer, and an adviser to political sachems in trying times. It was widely thought that he should enter public life, and some tempting offers were made to him, even by the New Deal administration in Washington, but at the last moment he always found himself too engrossed in guiding his beloved firm to be able to tear himself away.

On the domestic side his life was not quite so easy. Three daughters were born to him and Hetty, but no son, and after the difficult delivery of the third it was thought medically inadvisable for Hetty to undergo another pregnancy. Lavinia, or "Vinnie," a bold beauty, soon became her father's particular pride and joy, easily outdistancing her less interesting younger siblings, though they were amiable enough and pretty enough, but lacking in her fire. Oh yes, he cared for them all, if he favored Vinnie, but he yearned for a boy, a youth, an heir whom he could rear to be a hero — he allowed his private ruminations to be wildly romantic — avoiding all the errors into which his own parents had fallen. At times the very sharpness of his regret surprised him. Why should a priest of the life of reason make such a distinction between an unborn son and a very present daughter?

It was certainly something of which Hetty was very much aware. She turned her attention to making up to her younger daughters for their father's obvious favoritism, but try as she could, she couldn't quite help adding this parental fault to the largely hidden grudge that she held against him for so sorely missing a son. She herself would have willingly risked her life to provide him with one, but he would not hear of it and even discontinued sexual relations with her in fear of slipping up. Of course, she couldn't help but suspect that this was less of a sacrifice for him than for her, a suspicion more than confirmed when his abstinence survived her menopause. The years had not made her more attractive, and her new stoutness and thinning hair had destroyed much of what little sex appeal she had had for him.

Certainly, however, she did her job as the senior partner's wife very well. Nobody disputed that. In town, in their commodious brownstone with a butler and four maids, and in Glenville, in their handsome white colonial revival house, she was appreciated as a clever if sometimes sharp-tongued, efficient, busy little hostess, especially by the shy young wives of newly made partners whom she clucked over like a kindly mother hen. But there was a vein of repressed sadness, a touch of muffled grimness behind her rather bustling activity, even lurking in the jangle of her laughter. Hetty knew that the gamble she had taken in wedding a great man who cared less for her than for his own greatness would have paid off in full only if she had given him the family *he* wanted. She was fair enough to recognize that the gamble had been her option and that she had no one to blame but herself. But she wouldn't have been human if she didn't sometimes take it out on him.

THE SUMMER OF 1953 wrought havoc both inside and outside the firm of Vollard Kaye. Ambrose had never faced a personal emotional crisis as bewildering and upsetting as that caused him by his son-in-law's adultery. He could not seem to find, in the well-stocked armory of his selected resources, the tool to deal with it. He had always inwardly lauded himself on a precise understanding of what he liked to think of as his own highly individual and complex double personality. He had formulated a diagnosis of himself as a kind of Jekyll and Hyde —

eliminating, of course, the darkest evil of the latter — and he had practiced the inner therapy (harmless, as he had then believed) of dramatizing himself as two brilliant but near opposite types. One, of course, was the prominent public figure — large, bony, broad-shouldered, grizzled, high-browed and expensively tweeded, with hard gray eyes that, however, could twinkle as well as rebuke, a legal scholar and philosopher as well as a deft administrator, a lofty idealist who was yet capable of diplomatic compromise. The other was a man of concealed depressions, the victim of black moods in which he believed in nobody and nothing and would try to console himself behind the locked doors of his study at home with a bottle of whiskey. But there was also a horrid little spy in his psyche that whispered to him that his melancholia was the finishing touch that the first Ambrose Vollard needed for a properly dramatic portrait.

And now, due no doubt to the high pitch of his resentment of the man who had betrayed his favorite daughter — and her father, too, oh yes her father as well — a fourth Ambrose seemed to be emerging, a grotesque caricature of the whispering spy, a shrill hyena accusing the two other Vollards of playing God and Satan in their own Paradise Lost. Was he having a true nervous breakdown at last?

He recalled with searing clarity the image of the twenty-three-year-old Rodman Jessup who had first applied for a job in Vollard Kaye in the fall of 1939. Under the high-standing wavy blond hair was a beautiful boyish face, the face of a fine clean youth, a kind of all-American cartoon. Yet the eyes had a mature and rather fixed stare, and one felt that the muscular, well-shaped body under the white spotless summer suit would respond instantly to anything those eyes saw as needing correction.

Ambrose had been half apologetic about the exiguous salary then customarily offered to law school graduates.

"Oh, that's quite all right, sir," was the prompt response. "I'm looking for opportunity more than remuneration. I've had to work my way through college and law school, and I'm used to making do with small means. And if I may say so, sir, it was hearing you address my graduating class at Yale three years ago that made me apply first to your firm. I've never forgotten the way you pictured the high role that lawyers can play in our business system."

Ambrose looked at him carefully for a moment. Was this flattery? "My daughter Lavinia is a friend of yours, I believe. She told me that you were going to apply here."

"I am honored if she describes me as a friend, sir. But I hadn't intended to mention her name to you. The only endorser I bring is myself."

"Plus a very good record at Columbia Law. Not to mention your editorship in the Journal. I was an editor myself."

"As all our board well knew, sir."

"How did you happen to pick Columbia over, say, Harvard?"

"I was able to get a partial scholarship there. And by living with my mother here in town I could save board."

Of course, Rodman was immediately hired — he was clearly something of a catch. But what clinched the matter was something that Ambrose already knew and that the applicant did *not* know: that Vinnie had already confided in her father that she had every intention of bringing the young Jessup to the point of proposing to her.

Ambrose had succumbed to the somewhat perverse temptation to submit this self-assured intruder into his family midst to the toughest office test, so he assigned the new recruit to the job of acting as his principal assistant in the most complicated of corporate reorganizations. Rod had been extraordinary. He toiled away, night and day, even sleeping on a couch in the law library, until he mastered every detail of the massive transaction with a clarity of mind and an organizing capability that had astonished and delighted his new boss. When the job was finished Ambrose took him out to a Lucullan dinner at the most expensive French restaurant in town, where, he was pleased to note, his guest partook freely of three famous wines without slurring a syllable.

As they sat over their cognac after their meal, Ambrose embarked on a more personal note. "Well, my boy, now you've had a glimpse of what a corporate law practice is all about, I daresay it strikes a young idealist like yourself as something a bit dustier than you'd expected. Even a bit grubbier. Isn't that so? You know the poem of the young Apollo, tiptoe on the verge of strife? How does it go? 'Magnificently unprepared for the long littleness of life'? Well, I suppose the 'magnificently' is something."

"But what are the details, sir, if the whole is good?"

"You find a corporate reorganization good? You interest me."

"Isn't it part of the social machinery that got us out of the great Depression? How can that not be good?"

"Well, I guess you might argue that in the matter we've just finished. But I'm afraid, my friend, you'll find that some reorganizations have no purpose loftier than to establish the control of one set of pirates over another."

Ambrose, facing the cool responding stare of those blue-gray eyes, felt almost ashamed of himself. What was he up to now, old ham that he was, but trying to impress this young man with the broad reach of a mind that could dive into the bottom as well as rise to the top of a modern law practice?

"But those things are going to be done anyway, sir" was Rod's sturdy reply. "As I see it, our job is to make sure they are done efficiently and lawfully. In a democracy, and in a free market, or as free as practicable, we have to allow businessmen to some extent to work things out their own way. But as lawyers we can see that they work it out strictly within the law. It doesn't matter so much *what* they do, as long as it's in the public eye. Then, if laws have to be changed, the voters will know what to change."

Ambrose nodded musingly. "Which means that a lawyer doesn't really need a conscience at all?"

"Or the highest and most sensitive kind. Like your own, sir."

This had all been very gratifying, and the young man was evidently sincere, if almost too much so. It had not taken more than a few months before it was recognized by all twenty partners and sixty clerks that young Jessup had been enlisted among the small group of selected associates who worked almost exclusively for the senior partner. Within a year Rod had become Ambrose's son-in-law, and in another five he was made the youngest member of the firm. A tour of naval duty in the Pacific in World War II only added to his luster, and he and Vinnie, neighbors of her parents in town and tenants of a cottage abutting the latters' estate in Glenville, became as essential to Ambrose's family as they were to his law practice. Even Vinnie's younger sisters adored their handsome and intriguingly serious brother-in-law and sought his approval of their boyfriends.

There were times when Ambrose liked to think of himself as an aging Hadrian leaning on the sturdy shoulders of a stalwart Antinoüs, on whose total fidelity he could confidently rely to help him bear the burdens of empire. But there were also moments when he was subject to the uncomfortable suspicion that his protégé was gaining control of his inner being and becoming as much a guide as a support. If there was the hint of a fanatic in Rod, there might also be the hint of a fanatic's strength.

When a vacancy on the Court of Appeals in Albany prompted gossip that the governor might appoint Ambrose to the seat, he discussed the pros and cons of his accepting it with Rod over lunch at the Downtown Association.

His son-in-law did not conceal his concern. "But what would happen to the firm?" he protested.

"Nothing. It would get along just fine. Nobody's indispensable. And there's a side of me that would like to philosophize about law for a bit. As judges can."

"How many judges do?"

"Well, call me Holmes, then!" Ambrose exclaimed with irritation. "Call me Cardozo! Can't there be anything in my life but the firm? Must I go to my grave having done nothing but represent more or less flawed characters? I want a moment of truth. Shining truth!"

Rod's retort was almost fierce. "But that's precisely what you have! You've forged this great law firm into your tool. Or rather into your shining sword! You say you're not indispensable to it, but I claim you are. There's not another firm in town with our unity, our spirit, and you are what holds the whole thing together. Every one of your partners feels the firm not only as his place of business, but as his club, his school, perhaps even his church!"

Ambrose at this chose to conclude the discussion, and anyway, as it turned out, the governor did not appoint him. But if he had, would Ambrose have turned it down? And would he have been doing it under the sway of Rod's so flattering estimate of his value to the firm? Wasn't it really time for him

41

to quit? Was it really good for any partnership to be so dominated by a single member? Oh yes, he tried to kid himself
that Vollard Kaye was as democratic as a Greek city-state, but
didn't he *know* that he was in fact a despot, however benevolent? And didn't he like it? Too much? And wasn't his present
nervousness possible evidence of a hidden fear that Rod Jessup
was grooming himself for the successorship but thought the
time was not yet quite ripe?

And then, only a few months before the dreadful event of the
flaunted adultery, came the first serious row in Ambrose's hal-
cyon relationship with his son-in-law.

One of the partners, exultantly, had just brought in an important new client, a large Canadian distilling corporation, and
Ambrose, immediately before his row with Rod, had been in
conference with some half dozen of the company's chief officers. He had been pleased with their reception and interested
in some of the problems they faced with Uncle Sam, to one of
which he had already flared a possible solution, and, finding
Rod in his office when he returned from the conference chamber, he started at once to explain it. But his son-in-law held up
an interrupting hand.

"I'm sorry to say it, sir, but I don't think you can represent
them."

"You mean we have a conflict? What a shame."

"Not a conflict, no. Though you could use our representing
Deacon Brewers, a potential litigant with them, as an excuse
for declining their retainer."

Ambrose stared. "And why should I want to do that?"

"Because they're crooks. Or at least used to be."

"Used to be?"

"Well, I don't suppose they could be criminally indicted
today for what they did thirty years ago. And it hasn't been

necessary for them to commit mayhem or murder since Prohibition was repealed."

"You mean they were involved in bootlegging back in the twenties and thirties? Good heavens, man, who wasn't? What do you think we're running here on Wall Street? A reformatory?"

"I'm not talking about just bootlegging. I'm talking about gang warfare and brutal murder." Rod had declined to sit down when Ambrose did; he loomed threateningly over the latter's desk and even struck its surface with his fist. "It so happens that I wrote my senior thesis at Yale on just that. I got absorbed in the subject and did a lot of personal research, including reading the record of several court cases. It may interest you to know that your new client was up to its ears in all kinds of suspected dirty work and was even — though I admit it was never proved — widely believed to have instigated the slaughter of two rivals to its gang right here in Manhattan. One of the men was even supposed to have been burned alive."

Ambrose shuddered. Execution at the stake had been one of his recurrent nightmares. He remembered how in his college days he had bitterly ejected Sir Thomas More from his mental catalogue of historical heroes when he read that the so-called saint had ordered the burning of Anabaptists. Then he shook himself. "But all that's ancient history, Rod. Even if there were officers of the company mixed up in such doings, they must be long dead or retired. There's no point holding the past against perfectly innocent men today."

"But they're not all dead or retired! The president of the company whom you've just been conferring with, Stanley Foot, was directly involved as a young man in their cross-boundary operations. I even devoted a section of my thesis to him. There was an effort by our feds to indict him, but the smokescreen sent up by shysters reduced it to nothing. Oh, of course, he's the image of respectability now. He's even got a flock of honorary degrees!"

Ambrose uncomfortably recalled the stout, hearty features of the loud-mouthed, grinning and genial Mr. Foot, the essence of an assured, lower-middle-class cockney Britisher.

Rod continued. "I got so wrapped up in my thesis that I even thought of taking a year off before law school to develop it into a book. But Mother said we couldn't really afford it. In my opinion American morals have never fully recovered from the blow that era of lawlessness dealt them. I'm sure you will agree now, sir, that a lawyer of your standing at the bar cannot possibly represent such a man as Stanley Foot."

Ambrose rubbed his eyelids and sighed. "You're not suggesting, are you, Rodney, that any of the gentlemen with whom I have just been in conference are planning — or even contemplating — any such felonies as you have described?"

"Of course not. Their need for that is over. Now they can do everything according to Hoyle."

Ambrose ignored his qualification. "And, to your knowledge, do any of these gentlemen engage today in any business practices that are unlawful? Let me put it more strongly. Do they engage in any business activity that is even improper?"

"Not that I know of."

"You give them the benefit of a doubt, then?"

"If I must."

"Very handsome of you. Well, let me tell you, my friend, what you ought to know without my having to tell you: that the ethics of the bar do not require me to turn my back on a prospective client for sins he may have committed in the past. This goes even more strongly for unproven sins of the very distant past. My only duty is to assure myself of the legality of his present operations. Under any other criterion a host of men might find themselves unable to find counsel. The world is full of closets and closets full of skeletons!"

"But surely, sir, when you *know* what this man did and got away with! Can you doubt he'd do it again if he thought his business required it?"

"I don't *know* anything, Rodman. And I'm not going to speculate what goes on in Mr. Foot's mind."

"But if I could convince you, sir! I've still got my old college notes —"

"I'm not interested."

"Then you close your eyes to murder and mayhem! Sir, I would never have believed it of you!"

"Now you're being impertinent. I must ask you to leave my office before you say anything further that you may regret."

Rod was livid now. "I'll not only leave this room, sir. I'll leave the firm!" And he turned abruptly to the door.

"Rod!" Ambrose cried, rising from his seat. "Rod, you can't mean it!"

"Oh, but I do, sir. I cannot remain a member of a firm that represents Stanley Foot!"

And he departed.

Ambrose spent the afternoon in his office, the door shut, refusing to see anyone or to take any calls. It was like a two-hour drowning, and his life crossed and recrossed his mind several times. In the end he called in his secretary and dictated a memorandum to Rodman authorizing him to inform the new Canadian client that they regretted very much that they could not accept their retainer because of a conflict of interest.

THE THREATENED RESIGNATION that Rod, the too strict interpreter of legal ethics, now no longer had to offer to his senior was soon followed by the actual resignation of Rod, the adulterer. Ambrose couldn't recall a crisis in his life where he had been so hard put to bring the diverse elements to his wrath and consternation into any kind of coherent order. Why could he not seem to get to the root of the fury that Rod's betrayal aroused in him? Or was the answer that he *could* get to its root? His anger, he had to reluctantly concede, was not really on behalf of his daughter or of her two little daughters, or even, as he wanted to think, on behalf of the firm. It was on behalf of himself alone.

Now what did this mean? Of course, he knew what it would mean to a slyly smirking, lewdly winking world. It would mean that his feeling for Rod was a homosexual obsession, and that his private image of himself as Hadrian and Rod as the beloved Antinoüs was only too exact. Yet he had never been conscious of a desire of any kind of physical intimacy with the younger man; he had hardly ever so much as patted him on the back. Of course, he had read too much not to be aware of the powers of repression that can drive such impulses from the conscious mind, but if they are that deeply hidden, can they really be said to exist? He had preferred to see himself as an ancient Greek of the highest Socratic type whose sensual needs were satisfied by women but whose spiritual ones craved the company of idealistic younger men. He had even rather fancied himself in that role.

He found some consolation in talking over the problem of how to handle Rod with the only person in the office who seemed to have all the threats in hand. Harry Hammersly was almost Rod's equal in brilliance, a seemingly confirmed bachelor and the intimate friend of both Rod and Vinnie. His tall straight figure, square brow and shiny black hair might have suggested a formidable virility had his air not been mitigated by a kind of self-deprecating smile, too much hearty laughter at the mildest jokes of others and a conversational habit of self-mockery.

Ambrose had consulted Harry before accepting Rod's resignation from the firm. He felt that the value of his son-in-law's legal services was too great to be dispensed with on his say-so alone. But Harry had seen no alternative.

"You know what pals Rod and I have always been, so you can imagine, sir, what pain it gives me to say what I have to say. Rodney will be regarded by many, perhaps most, of our partners as one who has offended you, and consequently themselves, beyond the scope of any real forgiveness. The spirit of unity which has been one of your greatest contributions to the firm would be fatally shattered if you kept him on. And you needn't be concerned about Rod's future. He will find another good post soon enough. No doubt with one of our rivals."

Ambrose nodded slowly as he took this in. "And how do you think I should advise my afflicted daughter? I know she has a loyal friend in you, Harry."

"I am proud to hear you say it, sir. Of course, a divorce is necessary. Your pride and hers could hardly consider a reconciliation under the circumstances, even if one were offered, which seems most unlikely."

"I have to agree with that."

"And in choosing the jurisdiction in which to sue, I see no reason to look beyond the borders of the state in which the wrong occurred and which happens to be the true domicile of both parties."

"You mean here in New York? On the grounds of adultery? Do you want a scandal greater than the one we already have? What are you talking about, Harry?"

"I'm talking about what we can do for Rod, sir. Something

47

that may help to thrust him back into the senses he seems temporarily to have lost. What the psychiatrists call shock treatment, except we needn't use electricity. Let him see in the newspapers his spades called spades, his paramour named, his sin defined. Why should we smooth it all over for him in a Reno fantasy where we ask for a decree because he trumped his partner's ace at the bridge table? We owe it to Rod, as a man we have loved and respected, to show him just how low he has sunk. And maybe that will help him get back on his feet."

Ambrose could hardly swallow. His throat was choked, until he coughed several times and then wiped his eyes. Had he allowed the image of Rod as the man he himself had always yearned to be — direct, straightforward, devoid of dark doubts and intrusive conceits — so to seize his mind and soul that Rod's apostasy seemed the suicide of Ambrose Vollard?

"Well, Harry, there may be justice in what you say."

He knew he would have to discuss the matter with his wife, and he did so that night after dinner, when they were having their coffee in the library. She clearly knew something of the sort was coming as she sat, impassive, enigmatic, on the other side of the fireplace.

"You seem unusually Zeus-like tonight, my dear," she offered at last. "When may I expect the first thunderbolt?"

Ambrose used to tell his friends, only half jocularly, that Hetty exceeded Browning's last duchess in that her smiles, or rather her cackling laughs, went everywhere, but particularly in his direction, so that, had he been a Renaissance despot, he might have given "commands" to muffle her.

Somewhat gruffly now he summarized his discussion with Hammersly.

"Harry recommends a New York divorce?" she queried in dismay. "And we thought he and Rodman were such pals!"

"He's thinking of Vinnie. Why should the poor child have to

take herself to some godless western state and swear falsely that she resides there, when our own legislature in Albany has provided the just and effective remedy for the wrong she has suffered?"

"Why? To avoid a stinking scandal, that's why."

"The scandal is already here. Our son-in-law has taken care of that."

"But you'd make it worse. And don't talk to me about false swearing. Your firm has sent plenty of clients to Reno, including your niece, Stuffy's child, who had the same grounds of complaint as Vinnie."

"That was different."

"It was different in that you had no particular resentment against her husband. You just wanted to get rid of him, that was all. And she had another fool ready to marry her."

"Which is hardly Vinnie's case."

"What do you really know about Vinnie's case? Rod is what's got you so worked up. I've never seen you so violent."

"And what about you?" he demanded, raising his voice to take the offensive. "Wouldn't a little violence become a mother whose daughter has been so foully treated? But no, you can never lose your cool. I daresay you think Rod is only behaving as most men would, given half a chance. Isn't that part of your creed of cynicism?"

Hetty cut through his reproaches to make a single point. "I don't think Rod is behaving at all like other men. He's basically a puritan. Maybe it takes a Bostonian to see that."

"Well, he's certainly not acting like a puritan."

"But maybe he's reacting like one. A puritan turned inside out."

"A puritan gone to the devil, you mean?"

"That could be it. Maybe he hasn't learned that if God is dead, the devil must be, too."

"Which is taking us a long way from choosing the forum for the divorce."

"Oh, if you're determined to get one, I don't really care where. And I suppose a divorce is inevitable. You don't hear much these days of reconciliations. The first thing that goes wrong in a marriage and, bang, call the lawyer. And after that it's hopeless."

"The bar has always enjoyed your good opinion, my dear."

It had been easy to predict that Hetty's reaction to the proposed jurisdiction of the divorce would irritate him, but Vinnie's came as a surprise. She seemed upset and fidgety during their conference in his office the next day, and twice rose to walk to the window and contemplate the view. He thought she looked a bit haggard, certainly less pretty than usual, which he hated, for her looks were important to him. The big blond girl with the laughing blue eyes and radiant smile had become plumper with the years, not in the least to make her unattractive but enough to take her out of the category of beauties in which he had once so proudly placed her. He couldn't understand why his motherly old secretary, Mrs. Peck, insisted that Vinnie's increased avoirdupois had made her rounder and "sexier."

Vinnie uttered a little cry when he came to the point about the New York divorce.

"You side with Harry, then?"

"I most certainly do."

"Well, if you both agree, I suppose I must go along. I know Mummy's against it, but then Mummy's always basically neutral, and she doesn't really care. I've been brought up all my life to think of Vollard Kaye as something that could never be wrong. As a kind of holy tribunal. Like King Arthur's round table. Where all the knights were perfect gentlemen and invincible fighters. And Rod as Lancelot. And now look what's happening. Lancelot's being thrown out of Camelot!"

"Not for an affair with King Arthur's wife, anyway," Ambrose couldn't help interjecting.

"Not with Mummy, hardly!" Here Vinnie broke into a kind of gasping laugh that shocked him. Had she been drinking? At ten o'clock in the morning? "No, he's more like Satan than Lancelot, isn't he? So he must be cast out of heaven, down, down, down . . ." She leaned over and stared at the floor.

"So there we are, my dear," Ambrose murmured in a softer tone, beginning to be alarmed at her uncharacteristic mood.

"Well, I guess I must do as I'm told, Daddy. One rebellion in Vollard Kaye is surely enough for one year."

"Vinnie! You're beginning to sound like your mother."

4

Vɪɴɴɪᴇ ᴀᴛ ᴠᴀssᴀʀ in the late nineteen thirties had been a happy and lucky young woman, and happier and luckier in that she knew she was both. A beauty — or near beauty — she enjoyed radiant health, a handsome allowance, and the college courses in literature and creative writing that had captured her imagination. She lived in a world where women were coming into their own and contemplating full-time careers, though those of her generation, at least in the eastern seaboard upper strata, were still largely of a mind that raising a family came first. The country had come through a dark Depression, and the economic sun was again rising, and shrill dictators in Rome, Berlin and Moscow, however tiresome, were not yet overclouding the European horizon. Between us and them still bristled the royal navy and France's standing army.

And, as her father's all but acknowledged favorite, Vinnie ruled the roost at home. It was her mother's option to remain on the sidelines, content to criticize rather than lead, supplying a role not unlike that of the Roman sage who stood directly behind the general in the chariot leading a triumph to remind him that he was still a mortal. Vinnie thought she more than made up for this by extolling her father as a god, *her* god. She reveled in their intimate companionship, in sharing his problems in the leadership of his firm, in the turmoil of his visiting doubts, even in his relationship with her mother, confident that he loved her not only more than anyone else in his life but in a way that was different from any in which he had loved before. She sensed the emptiness that his own mother's indifference had left in him, and fancied that she could fill it, not only for his but for her own advantage. For what was the benefit of having a great father if some of that greatness did not rub off on her? Could such a supposition be called egotistical when it was just what he wanted himself?

Hetty Vollard tended to regard her eldest daughter's idolization of her father, and his of her, as something of a relief, as if it reduced her maternal responsibilities from three to two. She could turn her attention to making up to the younger daughters for any deficiencies in the paternal concern, which was not difficult as Ambrose's general amiability and kindness with all his progeny cloaked much of his preference for Vinnie. This did not deter Hetty, however, from being sarcastic among her lady friends over such a preference, describing it as a Victorian pastel of the benevolent aging sire stroking the golden hair of the lovely child who knows just how to get around him. Couldn't one see it, she would ask laughingly, as the idealized union of the sexes, with the male providing strength and protection, and the female fidelity and love? Wasn't that the bargain that assured the female of an unproclaimed but necessary dominion? Union of the sexes? No, abolition of sex! Wasn't that what a true civilization required?

Vinnie had never quite understood her mother, but she welcomed her detachment as she feared her tongue. She saw how other girls controlled their mothers by turning down or even off the daily show of affection the latter seemed to need, but her mother did not appear to have any such necessity. Her father, of course, was just the opposite, at least where she was concerned, and she did not hesitate to draw heavily on the large balance of love that he kept in store for her. She had, indeed, love to return to him, but her love went hand in hand with a shrewd assessment of his character and motives. She understood and went along with his habit of dramatizing himself to himself. But she also appreciated the large scope of his mind and its outreaches — she deemed him to know everything from the earliest Saxon law to dadaism — and she conceived of it as a sacred duty — made more sacred by her mother's patent neglect of it — to be an acolyte at his altar. An acolyte, of course, could rise in the world, could be a cardinal or an éminence grise to a king, couldn't he?

The question of her debutante party offered the perfect opportunity for filial maneuvering. Vinnie knew that a hotel ballroom had to be reserved long in advance, and it was necessary to remind her father of this. She brought up the subject at the breakfast table. For a minute he seemed disinclined even to answer her, engrossed in his *Times* editorial.

"Are you sure you really want this party?" he growled at last. "To me it's like throwing the money in the East River."

"Isn't it expected of me?"

"Expected of you? What do you want to be, the slave of fashion? And an idiot fashion, at that. How about setting an example to bust the inane custom of spending a small fortune on a single night's revel to introduce one's daughter to a list of idle young men, provided by a professional party giver, among whom one devoutly hopes she will *not* select a husband! Why, the other day, at my lunch club, they were talking about a family who actually allowed their son to quit college so they could pay for his sister's ball!"

Vinnie paused coolly to assemble arguments that she knew

would dispose of his objections. "Of course, I don't want any party if you think you can't afford it, Pa. Or even if you're going to worry about the cost. You've done enough for me already. More than enough."

This had its effect. "It's not so much the cost, my dear. I can handle that. And I haven't done a thing for you that you haven't well deserved. It's just the idea of the thing that bothers me. Doesn't it sometimes bother a bright girl like you?"

"Of course it does. I'd be horrified if I had a brother who gave up college for my party. But that boy's family must have been a very silly one. I don't see much point worrying about people like that."

"You have a point there."

"And if people who can afford it, give their daughter a coming-out party, is there really so much harm in it? Look at all the other crazy ways they spend their money!"

"I can't deny that."

"Of course, if I don't have a party, I shan't be able to go to any others."

Her father looked up from his paper now. "Why does that follow?"

"Well, think of it, Pa. If I took a high stand about the idiocy of debutante parties and still went to them, everyone would say I was a hypocrite. And what's more, that it was just a pose on my part to cover my family's stinginess in not giving me one of my own."

"That wouldn't have to follow at all."

"But you know it would. Anyway it doesn't matter, because I shan't really mind giving up the silly party." As she sensed the paternal crumbling she warmed to the game. She thought of the proposed new common room for the settlement house of which her father was a trustee and where she and her sisters

55

sometimes put in an hour or so, angels of light, playing games with the children in the day care center. She had a vision of the explosive gratitude of all at a sudden unexpected donation and the immediate board resolution to name the new acquisition the Lavinia Vollard Room. "Why, the money saved might even pay for your new addition to the settlement house! You could call off your fund drive!"

Ambrose thrust his newspaper aside. "And supposing, Vinnie, I put it to you that I'd pay for that room with the money I'd save on your party, if you were really willing to give it up?"

"Pa! Are you serious?"

"Never more so!"

"Then I'd say yes, do it!"

"On one condition. That you agree to go to all your friends' coming-out parties. And, of course, you'll have one of your own, as well. Perhaps not quite as spiffy as it would have been without the expense of the new room, but spiffy enough."

"Oh, Pa!"

Vinnie rose to fling her arms around her father's neck while her younger sisters clapped. After he had left the table to go to work, accompanied by her sisters en route to school, she was left alone to finish her coffee with her mother, who had not contributed a word to the discussion.

"That was very neatly done, Lavinia," was Hetty's first dry comment.

"How do you mean, neatly?"

"Of course, you knew that by suggesting a charitable use of the party money, you'd get the ball as well. And far from being less spiffy, it will be one of the grandest of the season. Oh, your father will see to that. He's enchanted with your philanthropy."

"Oh, Mummy, you always see the low side of things. Can't you give a daughter some credit for even a smitch of generosity?"

"I give you more for insight, my dear. You're a clever girl. But even so, there are some things you don't see. Something you didn't see just now, for example."

"And that is?"

"That your father was perfectly aware of what you were up to."

"He thought I was putting it on?"

"He *knew* you were putting it on. He *liked* you for putting it on. What he really admires is the appearance of generosity and unselfishness. Your father has a great respect for appearances. Why not? Aren't they really what civilization is made of?"

"Oh, Mummy, there you go."

"Because I don't play the mother-daughter game? The way you play the father-daughter one? I'm sorry to have to tell you, child, but you do overdo it. I may admire the play, but I have to be concerned with what will happen when the curtain falls."

Vinnie said nothing to this; she simply left the table. She had learned not to pursue a topic too closely when her mother was in one of her "moods." There was a bleakness that Hetty seemed to have brought from New England climes that dulled even the dancing sunlight on the pavements of Manhattan. Deprived of the roasting faith of Dr. Shattuck's perfervid religiosity, his daughter's had dwindled to a rather chilling transcendentalism.

There was one snag for Vinnie in what her mother called the father-daughter game. She hated the idea that if her father had had a son, that son, unless he'd been a hopeless dunce or an irredeemable rotter, would surely have taken her place in the paternal adoration. He would have become a lawyer, of course, and the heir to the holy firm. Vinnie had had no ambition to join the bar; in her generation female attorneys were still rare, and Vollard Kaye numbered not even one in its roster. After college she had elected a rather leisurely postgraduate course at Columbia, applying for a master's in English lit. But she had always regarded with somewhat jealous eye the different young law associates whom her father seemed to favor, and when he brought one of them to Glenville for a weekend — usually devoted at least in part to brief writing — she had flirted rather shamelessly with the poor man in his few free hours. She derived a mild satisfaction from thus purloining a possible protégé from the grip of her powerful parent. But none of these flirtations amounted to much; the young man in question was often already engaged, and sometimes even married. The only way for her to get around the snag of a rival to herself in her father's love was the crude and obvious one of producing a son-in-law whom she could control even as he controlled her sire.

She met Rodman Jessup in her last year at Vassar at a cocktail party in New York, and she had been immediately attracted by his striking good looks and grave demeanor. He seemed to know few in the room — the party, she learned later, was given by the parents of his law school roommate — and he stood rather aside in a corner but without the least air of constraint. When Vinnie asked the daughter of the house about him, she was told, sarcastically, that he was the "strong silent type" and she asked if that wasn't "what we all want," particularly the silence. But introduced, she did not find him so quiet. They talked about Hitler's occupation of the Rhineland, and he was very emphatic indeed about the need for immediate armed resistance. When he found that she agreed with him, he, rather surprisingly, invited her to have dinner with him at a cafeteria, announcing firmly that he couldn't afford a "fancier spot," and she heard herself, also rather surprisingly, accept.

At their table she asked him about law school and mentioned that her father was a lawyer.

"And one of the greats!" he exclaimed with an enthusiasm obviously genuine. "He spoke at my Yale graduation. Oh, I really stared at that party when I heard you were Ambrose Vollard's daughter."

She was amused but also pleased. "Is that why you asked me out?" And her question was frank, not coy.

"It was why I stared. Not why I asked you out. That was after we'd talked."

"Oh, then I was on my own."

"And a very beautiful own it was."

Her first reaction, that he was a pretty fast worker, was suddenly mitigated by her odd sense of his total honesty. She began to suspect that this young man was not a callow male looking for a quick smooch, but a creature of strong reserve and chivalrous good manners on whom her own appeal had made an unprecedented assault. But what grounds had she for so grossly flattering an estimate of her own charms? Few. She was bewildered.

"Tell me about yourself," was what she finally said.

He was only too willing to do this. He spoke warmly, even glowingly, about his parents, whose only child he was. His father had died when Rodman was fourteen, of a heart ailment, cutting short a brilliant law career that might have taken him to high office, and leaving his widow and son a sadly exiguous capital, the result of his habit of taking too many cases of a public interest on a pro bono basis.

"My father was all heart," he explained. "But he knew that his physical one was weak and that he might not live to see me grow up. The one thing he wanted to make sure of was that I should live my own life and make my own decisions. 'Never feel you have to follow in my footsteps or do anything because I have done it. Be your own man, sonny, and tell yourself that I'm always right there behind you. In spirit if not in flesh. And never regret our little quarrels. I've enjoyed them as much as you have.'"

"But you did go into the law, after all," she pointed out. "Are you sure it was entirely your own decision?"

"It was certainly mine in a way. Except you might say it had been made for me. Father was so much a part of me that it seemed almost inconceivable that I could choose any profession but his. And there was poor Mother, too. I lost her only last year. She had dedicated herself wholly to his memory. Too much so, I'm afraid. She was so bitter about his golden career cut short that she couldn't seem to reconcile herself to a fate that had done it."

"I suppose she wanted you to make it up to her in some way. That would have been only natural."

"But she was always fair. She knew I had to live my own life and that she couldn't share it as she had shared Father's."

"No. For that you'd have to find another *her.*"

"I should be so lucky," he said gravely and gave her a long look.

She changed the subject then and told him some of the story of her own life.

That summer she had three dates with him. She would have had more, had she not joined her family on a trip to Quebec. On none of those occasions was there a romantic interchange, but she certainly came to accept him as a beau. She was fairly confident that she could elicit almost any proposal from him the moment she wanted to, but she wasn't in the least sure that she was so minded. He was . . . well, how could she put it? Not at all like the other men she knew. And she was not yet ready to introduce him or even mention him to her father. For the time being, anyway, she was keeping him to herself.

"Of course, you're going to apply to Vollard Kaye for a job," she told him one night at their Automat.

"You think they'd take me?" he inquired earnestly. "I'm not exactly a white shoe type. And I'm told that most of the partners are listed in the Social Register."

"That's because most of them have worked their way up. Pa doesn't give a hoot about those distinctions. I thought you knew that."

"Oh, I wasn't thinking of *him*. To work for him would be my dream of dreams!"

"Please! You'll be making me think I'm only a rung in your ladder to fame."

He became instantly solemn. "You couldn't think anything as awful as that, could you, Vinnie?"

"Why not? A talented man without a fortune has to look about him to get started. In Europe it's taken quite for granted that one of the functions of a woman is to have something to give a push-up to a man, whether it be blood or connections or just hard cash."

"Vinnie, I don't want you to talk that way. Those things have nothing to do with how I feel about you. Tell me that you believe that, Vinnie. Tell me, please."

She was a bit taken aback by his gravity, but decided to pass it off. "Of course. I was only joking."

She discovered that his stern morality was absolutely consistent. He had no use for ambiguities or double standards. A discussion they had after attending a Saturday matinee of *Hedda Gabler* brought this out rather too forcibly for her. It was a play that had excited Vinnie, an Ibsen enthusiast, but which had failed to arouse Rodman on this, his first experience with the great Norse playwright.

"What does it all add up to?" he wanted to know. "A bored, idle woman in a fit of petty jealousy burns the manuscript of a presumably great book by a drunken genius and then goads him into suicide. After which she follows in the same godforsaken path. Is that a tragedy? Or even a comedy?"

Vinnie tried to recall the lecture of a favorite Vassar professor. "It's neither. You might call it an ancient morality play. Of man and morals, and a world outside of man and morals."

"What kind of a world is that?"

"We don't know! That's what's so spooky. Ibsen seems to believe in something like the survival of the old pagan gods. They lurk in the dark air around us. Old wild demiurges. Wasn't there a medieval legend that Dionysus reappeared in a monastery in the form of an impish youth and presided over orgies? Hedda is subject to some terrible influence like that. She has great force and will, but she is completely unrestrained by any modern sense of right or wrong."

"But she knows she's doing a wrong thing when she burns that manuscript," he objected. "She gives her husband a false excuse to explain what she's done."

"That's just to shut him up. She recognizes that other people know right from wrong. She even despises them for it. You must see her as a wild creature caged in a zoo of Victorian morality."

"Victorian? Is it Victorian to disapprove of destroying works of genius and handing loaded pistols to depressed alcoholics?"

"Well, call it man-made morality."

"Man-made! As opposed to what, Vinnie?"

"Oh, I don't know." She waved a hand vaguely in the air. "Maybe Ibsen is saying that other systems and values exist beside the frail ones that man has put together to separate himself from the beasts. They aren't necessarily what we would call nice ones."

"Well, if he means that, why doesn't he say it?"

"Because he's dealing with imponderables. With mysteries."

"Well, all I can see is that he's dealing with a wicked woman who gets what's coming to her in the end. There's your moral, I suppose. But wouldn't it be better to redeem her? To make her see the error of her ways? Isn't it rather crass the way he handles her? Sets her up and then knocks her down?"

"Certainly, the way *you* put it."

"I don't see any other way to put it. I can't see that it's any halfway excuse for her to say she was worshiping Dionysus or Bacchus or whoever, if that's what Ibsen *is* saying. There was a minister at school who used to preach a sermon about what he called overtolerance. 'Boys,' he used to say, 'you'll hear a lot of excuses these days for the bad things people do. You will hear that they are manic, or neurotic, or obsessed, or whatever. Don't forget, boys, one useful little word in your vocabulary. Wicked. Those people are wicked.' That may sound harsh to you, Vinnie, but it's really not. It's really kinder. Because the wicked can be redeemed. Isn't redeeming them better than explaining them?"

It struck Vinnie that his features had none of the dark, comminatory look that his words might have conjured up in another. He took no visible pleasure in the idea of stern judgment or punishment. If he was a knight, he was a knight like Galahad, more intent on rescue than revenge.

"I suppose if we go to *A Doll's House* next week — it's alternating with *Hedda* — you'll say that Nora should have stayed home and raised the children. And you might be right, too. Poor little things, look at the father she leaves them with."

And she came to the happy conclusion that he was not a man to slam doors but to open them.

But then, all at once, everything changed for her. Rod's roommate's family had a house in Glenville not far from the Vollards, and when Rod came down for a weekend visit there

Vinnie drove over to join him at their pool. He was clad in tight white swimming trunks, and for one blinding moment as she caught sight of him she thought he was naked. His skin was an ivory white, unlike the tanned bodies of the others at the poolside, for unlike them he had been cloistered in the city, but his torso, his shoulders, his thighs, finely sculpted, were splendid. She was confronted no longer with an overworked law student, a pale library product, but a magnificent man. She noted the sizable bulge in his pants where they covered his genitalia.

What now crawled over her like a massive skin itch was such a lust as she had never conceived herself having. She felt giddy, shocked. She was not only confronted with a new Rodman Jessup but a new Lavinia Vollard. She was going to have to reckon with a totally new force within herself.

Sitting beside him at the far end of the pool to which they both repaired, she found her mind so stuffed with sexual images that she had to find an outlet in a subject somehow related. She found herself telling him of a Vassar classmate who, finding herself pregnant at the termination of a wholly clandestine love affair, had availed herself of an abortion, without telling her family. He was visibly shocked. She should have had the child, he argued.

"But it would have been her social ruin," Vinnie protested. "She wanted to go on with her life as before, the way her ex-lover was doing. Of course, no one would have blamed him, even if it had become known."

"*I* would have blamed him. Just as much as I blame her. Even more, perhaps, because as a man he should have been stronger against temptation."

Vinnie debated for a moment in her mind. Was this naïveté or something finer? Had this near naked sleek animal been reserved for her alone? Her giddiness returned. "You hold that a man should keep himself as pure as a woman?"

"If he expects it of her, yes. Why should he have any lesser obligation?"

"And that he should be a virgin until he marries?"

"As much as his wife, anyway."

"But what about the old theory that he should have enough experience to initiate his bride in the rites of love?"

"Does it take so much experience? The birds and the bees don't seem to think so."

"They haven't been petrified by civilization. They haven't had to wear clothes."

"You think Adam and Eve had an easier time? Of course, they had no alternative to each other. Anyway, I don't think you'll find me lacking in that respect if you marry me."

"Heavens!" she gasped. "Is this a proposal?"

"It would be, if there were any chance of its being accepted."

"Too soon, too soon," she murmured, almost breathless at his precipitation. When he wasn't looking serious, he was almost too light. But there was no mistaking the yank at her heart. She had brought this man into her life, and she was going to have to cope with him. "I need more time, my friend. Only don't think I'm letting you off the hook. I shall remember that you have made a formal proposal."

"It's not binding, of course, until accepted. And it must be accepted or rejected within a reasonable time. How long shall we give it?"

"Say a year?"

But it only took months. They were married after his graduation from law school, during the first year that he worked at Vollard Kaye. Her father, delighted at the match, supplemented Rodman's slender salary, and they were soon settled very comfortably in a charming small flat in town. Rod, as a lover, proved indeed that he had no need of earlier amatory lessons, and there seemed no cloud on their wedding bliss.

Except a seemingly tiny one. Vinnie came to reflect that too much good luck and family approval might prove to have a faintly cloying side. One of her Vassar classmates had married a handsome Jewish boy who had helped her to her feet after a bad tumble on the Central Park skating rink. Her family shared the routine anti-Semitism of the then New York society, and his was stoutly Orthodox. Spurned by all four parents, the young couple had eloped in a frenzy of romantic delight and were promptly forgiven by both families on the birth of the first baby. Vinnie rather ruefully contrasted their Romeo and Juliet story with the heavy blanket of family congratulation that had almost stifled the pleasure of her engagement.

And in time there was something else. Rod from the beginning of their marriage had become more like a son than a son-in-law to her father. Wasn't this exactly what she had wanted? Oh, those gift-bearing Greeks! Had she immolated herself, a latter-day Iphigenia, on the altar of her father's frustrated paternity? In bringing him the son he craved, had she lost her own position in his heart?

Yet her marriage in every other way proved to be just what she had wanted. Rod worked joyfully and serenely in the firm and achieved not only an early partnership but the undisputed position of right hand to the man whom everyone referred to as the "chief." The year and a half that he spent in the Pacific on a destroyer only added to his glamour, and she loved reading his vivid letters aloud to her avidly listening (yes, even her mother!) family. Two little girls, in perfect health, were born to them, the product of her husband's regular and spirited, if somewhat predictable, lovemaking. And she had taken an active part in local charities, including her father's settlement house, and had become the admired chairman of the board of the Manhattan day school that her daughters attended.

And yet. When her father and husband, after a hearty Sunday lunch on a Glenville weekend, reverted to an animated discussion of their last corporate reorganization, she would sometimes find herself wondering if their Garden of Eden, which she had so tenderly planted and watered, was really open to either Eves or snakes. And if her function as a wife was not simply to supply the oil of a supporting love, both physical and spiritual, to the smooth working of an otherwise totally independent male machine. What imp was it in her that caused her fingers nervously to keep unraveling the far corners of the tapestry of her life? A tapestry that she had woven herself?

5

❧

WHAT WAS PERPLEXING to Vinnie was in how many ways Rod was the perfect spouse. That many of her girlfriends envied her she did not doubt. Not only was he a fine-looking and well-mannered man; she sensed that they presumed him to be a vigorous lover. And he was, though he went at it almost as if it were a regular and healthful calisthenic. He was definitely not open to imaginative variations of the act of coition, and the one time she had suggested a ritual described graphically to her by a girlfriend over a beach club sandwich, he had been distinctly shocked. After that she refrained from any further such suggestions and sought to content herself with the supple if habitual movements of his elegant body. How many women, after all, she would ask herself, had anything half as good as that?

And what was more, he was an easy man to live with. He was consistently good tempered, even when in the throes of a grinding securities case, and on the rare occasions when his mood darkened, he was considerately silent. He never reproached her for anything she did or failed to do. If something went wrong his rebuke was confined to a calm and reasonable suggestion of how it could be remedied. The children adored him, and no matter how many nights in the week he toiled at the office, a good part of every weekend was kept rigorously free to teach the girls tennis or take them sailing or, if it was raining, to a movie. He was a good host at their occasional Saturday night dinner parties, mixing drinks for all and never overindulging himself, looking after the shyer or less popular guests, showing a friendly interest in the pleasures or problems of all.

About herself and her own interests he was scrupulously careful to make inquiries as soon as he came home from the office. He interested himself in the fund-raising drives that she instituted for her settlement house and school, and offered her the names of clients to whom she might make an appeal. If it seemed to her that he was not deeply concerned with such matters, but lent a hand and ear solely because they were hers, was she not honest enough to admit that her own concern with them was not much greater? Even if she should raise enough money to allow the settlement house to divert and edify its whole neighborhood, or the school to endow chairs for the finest teachers and provide scholarships for all its needy students, would she enjoy a fraction of the high elation with which Rod approached each new law problem presented by a client? No! When she complained of this to her mother, for whose wisdom she sometimes hankered even as she feared its acidity, she found cold comfort indeed.

"If you want the thrill that men like your father and Rod get out of their profession, you have to go whole hog, my dear. That's what you and so many of your friends have yet to learn. The job must come first."

"You mean ahead of one's husband and children?"

"Oh yes. It might be better not to marry at all."

"Mother! You think I'd be happier if I'd been a lawyer?"

"Definitely. Or a dentist. Even an undertaker."

"And an old maid, to boot?"

"I don't know how you define an old maid. You could still have love affairs. Only they'd have to come second. The way they do with men. The best men."

The way they do with men! The words stuck in Vinnie's head. Was that true of all love? Even of Rod's? She was sure, if ever he were faced with having to make the unimaginable choice between herself and his law firm, that he would choose her. But would that really be love? Wouldn't it rather be duty? She knew, of course, that he could love, in his way, but wasn't duty the stronger force in him? Ah, that was the thing she didn't know about him, the inner Rod that had always eluded her, that eluded, she supposed, everybody, even her father. There was something that he grasped tightly to himself, guarding it, perhaps even unconsciously, from the whole world.

Where help came to her, if help it was, was from Harry Hammersly. He and Rod seemed to represent the attraction of opposites. Friends in college and law school and now law partners, they always remained in constant touch with each other. Yet Harry, a merry bachelor, was as mocking and impudent and charming as his pal was sober, polite and at times a bit grim. And if he made fun of the world, he made particular fun of Rod. Rod ordinarily did not appear to mind it, though he sometimes got a bit hot under the collar when Harry questioned the motives behind any legal position taken by the firm. On the whole, however, Harry, like a fool in a medieval court, was licensed, at least in Rod's domain, to say what he liked.

Vinnie had originally supposed that she should disapprove of Harry. His impudence verged on heresy, and he laughed at too many sacred things. But his apparent assumption that her wit and wide views lifted her to the level of isolated liberty, making them lonely partners in a world of amiable philistines whom it was their duty to entertain, was flattering. And his well-made but soft body, which she had initially found faintly repellent, even effeminate, she was bothered to find increasingly intriguing to her. The sensuous way he twisted his torso, particularly after making an off-color joke, she reluctantly admitted, titillated her. And in his rare moments of repose, as when he was listening to her — and a very attentive listener he could be — his almost handsome Roman face waxed almost noble, though he soon enough shattered the impression with his high screeching laugh, as though otherwise some deed of heroism might be horridly expected of him.

At length she began to suspect that there was something subtly undermining in the persistence of his jokes at her husband's expense. And that there might be something disturbing in her own acceptance of these.

One Sunday afternoon in Glenville, when the three of them were seated on the terrace by her father's tennis court after a game of singles between Rod and Harry, which Rod, of course, had won, the conversation fell on the trial of a famous gangster who was, surprisingly, represented by a respectable law firm. Vinnie asked whether Vollard Kaye would have taken such a case, and Rod firmly denied it.

"But doesn't even the most hardened criminal deserve a good defense?" she asked.

"Certainly. But hardened criminals, at least the rich ones, of whom, alas, there are only too many, can be very picky in choosing counsel. The problem, however, would never arise with us. No gangster would ever come knocking at *our* door. He'd know that his defense would be an absolutely honest one, with no dirty tricks. And that's the last thing he'd want."

"You imply that the firm representing the gangster in question is using dirty tricks?"

"If it deems them necessary, yes. We're not all perfect."

"Only Vollard Kaye?"

"Only Vollard Kaye." Rod smiled, as if to make the boast a jest, but she saw that he meant it well enough.

"I wonder," Harry now observed, "if we would be quite so pure if we didn't already have a plethora of less tainted fees. We can afford to dispense with dirty tricks. At least with the dirty tricks of the mob."

"You mean you have other kinds?" Vinnie asked.

"Oh, we have our nuances and innuendos."

"What do you mean by that?" There was just a hint of a snarl in Rod's tone.

"Oh, simply, my dear fellow, that we have the luxury of representing conquerors. *After* they have been all cleaned up and the blood washed away. Now that William the Norman is firmly settled on his throne we need not bother our pretty heads about how he obtained it."

"I suppose you're referring to the cutthroat methods of some of our nineteenth-century robber barons."

"Precisely. Were they not the predecessors of some of our most respectable corporate clients? And were not their counsel the predecessors of firms like ours?"

"You imply that we're no different from them?"

"I imply that it might take a mother's eye to spot the difference."

Rod's cheeks had taken on a tint of red. "You think, then, that if I'd been a lawyer in those days I'd have advised our railroad clients to buy legislatures and get around the rate limits with illegal kickbacks?"

"Not at all. You'd have been your clever self. You'd have been the master of the gentleman's cover-up and earned yourself as honorable a reputation as you have today. It was the name of the game, Rod!"

"You don't know me, Harry!"

Harry's smile simply broadened at this outburst. "Do I not?" He appealed to Vinnie. "You know the portrait of your great-uncle de Peyster that hangs in our reception hall? That perfectly tailored little gentleman with the trim goatee who seems to glance down at the visitors and wonder who let *them* in. Isn't there a hint of slyness behind that serene gaze? Well, Rod has improved on him. The mask is now perfect. The hint of slyness is quite gone! Welcome to the age of the knight-errant!"

When Vinnie laughed, which seemed to be what he was seeking, Harry hastened to mollify his friend. "Of course, my dear Rod, I was only pulling your leg. We all know you're true blue."

Sitting beside Harry a week later at one of her father's Sunday lunches, she decided to get a few things straight. In the mock serious tone one adopts when one is really serious, she asked him, "You don't believe in anything, do you, Harry? I mean in God or ethical principles or anything like that?"

"Well, I'm a positivist, if that's what you mean. It all has to be proved to me. I believe in taste. Good taste and bad."

"You mean as in interior decoration?"

"If you like. That's one aspect of it. I think it's bad taste to rob or murder or covet your neighbor's wife." Here he rolled his eyes comically. "Though I might be forgiven the last."

She did not comment on this. "And you certainly don't think it's good taste to keep lauding the sanctity of Vollard Kaye."

"I don't find my partners apostles, as some do."

"For some, read Rod Jessup?"

"Well, he certainly seems to find your father one."

"And you don't."

He laughed. "Oh, I admire him! He can thunder like Jehovah and grin like Satan. He's a primordial demiurge."

"I think Rod really worships him."

"Oh, Rod approaches him as the monkeys approach the rock python Kaa in *The Jungle Book*. But one day he'll come too close and get caught in those writhing coils."

"What do you mean by that?"

"You'll see, my dear. You'll see." And he ended the discussion by turning to the lady on his other side.

What Harry seemed to be dangling before her eyes was the flattering notion that she was not realizing her full potential, not living her own life to the full. And if one wasn't doing that, could one escape the suspicion that one wasn't really living at all? Had she been given all her blessings — and, ironically, weren't they just the blessings of which an earthly paradise was supposed to be full: a loving family, good health, money and social position? — simply that the imps of comedy might laugh at her?

She quite saw that Harry might be something bad. That there might be, after all, a snake in her Eden. But his companionship gave her the consolation of feeling she was not alone, that she had someone who understood and did not condemn her, because he, too, was being reminded by a conscience of all *he* had to be thankful for, because, in short, they were sort of spiritual twins, babes lost in an alien world.

"When people tell you to count your blessings," Harry told her, "it means they're on to you. They've sniffed out the fact that you don't appreciate all *they* have done for you. And they resent that. You're like a child on Christmas Day whose parents have substituted their own list for the one you left on the chimney for Santa."

"And that child was cheated!" she exclaimed. "It doesn't matter that the parents thought their list should have pleased her more."

She found herself trying to see Harry in a more positive

light. It wasn't so much, she sought to persuade herself, that he was tempting her to deny anything in her life; he was endeavoring, on the contrary, to make her realize that she needn't be ashamed of being a freer and more interesting specimen of humanity than the lot with whom fate had thrown her. So long as she didn't look down on these — and she didn't think she did — she could exchange an occasional wink with someone who found himself in the same boat. Yet she had to admit that Harry himself did sometimes look down on people. And one of those people, she was afraid, was Rod.

Harry didn't work as many nights in the office as Rod did, claiming that if one arrived at eight in the morning and stayed until seven at night and didn't "shoot the breeze" with fellow workers and take a two-hour lunch, one should be able to get all one's work done in the time allotted. The result was that he was often free to take Vinnie to plays or concerts to which she had tickets but to which, at the last moment, her husband was too busy to go. And sometimes he would take her afterwards for a nightcap to his elegant little duplex, the garden apartment of an old brownstone, to which he had a private entrance.

Listening to him as he took apart the old world of her lares and penates seemed to demonstrate to her that all her old doubts and reservations had not been merely the idle fancies that flutter through any unoccupied mind, but were substantial parts of her own being, and perhaps sinful parts as well. What made her almost welcome this belated, as she saw it, recognition of naughtiness was that it had a reality that her previous recognition, or fancied recognition, had lacked. She might be damned, but didn't one have to have been alive before one was damned? Wasn't it possibly worth it?

As her talks with Harry became more and more personal, he told her some of the problems of his private life. He had, the year before, broken off a long affair with a woman because she had wanted to marry him.

"But why didn't you marry her?" Vinnie had asked.

"Because I didn't love her."

"But, Harry, the time is coming when you ought to settle down. You're not twenty-one, my dear. Some men are not destined to fall head over heels in love. I don't think the greatest men are apt to feel passion in that way. Daddy, for example. I doubt if he ever really loved my mother. But you want to have a family and children, don't you?"

"With the right woman, yes."

"And what sort of woman is that?"

"Well, say a woman like you."

She didn't reply to this, and he didn't press the point. But they continued, on other occasions, to discuss sexual matters with what she liked to think was a clinical detachment, and in due course they came to an analysis of her own. Harry at last extracted from her the admission that she had never had sex with any man but Rod.

"I think it's a pity," he informed her blandly, "for any woman to be so limited. Far be it from me to say anything about Rod's performance in bed, which I'm sure is very fine, but there are joys in variety and experimentation, and in an ideal society I don't think any man or woman should be confined for life to a single mate. There ought to be ways of extending one's experience without incurring blame for broken vows. Indeed, that is why wife swapping is not an uncommon suburban practice."

"Really? Do you think it ever happens in Glenville?"

"I know damn well it happens in Glenville."

"Rod would die at the very idea."

"I agree that he would. So it could never happen to him. Anyway, I have no wife to offer him in return."

76

"And just what the hell do you mean by *that*?"

"My dear Vinnie, you know very well what I mean by that."

Which, of course, she did. Which, of course, they had been leading each other to. So here it was, right on the table. He did not try to fool her with any perfervid declaration of passion; he simply put it on the ground of a sensible, even a civilized, division of her life into what could be — with a little care, a little concern for the feelings and prejudices of others — a series of watertight compartments. There was no reason to believe, he now insisted to her, that what prudes called adultery had always to be found out. He knew of any number of cases, including couples of her acquaintance, where the so-called betrayed spouse remained in permanent and blissful ignorance of what was going on. Vinnie remained mostly silent on the occasions when he expounded his sexual philosophy, but her mind was afire with erotic images.

One night, while Rod was on a business trip to Chicago, Harry, after taking her to a movie and afterward to his flat for the usual nightcap, had retired, for an oddly prolonged time, to his bedroom, leaving her alone with her drink. When he suddenly appeared in the doorway, she gasped. He was clad only in a silk kimono with an unmistakable bulge at his crotch.

"Be not alarmed," he reassured her calmly. "No hand will be laid upon you. I am going to put on a record of the great duet from the second act of *Tristan*. It is, of course, notoriously the musical expression of the physical union of the lovers. I suggest that we listen to it in silence, after which you will be entirely free to choose your own finale. It can end in your stormy exit, like the bustle of King Mark, in which case I shall simply call you a taxi, or in our happier submission to what I am bold enough to call our most mutual attraction."

She thought he looked almost magnificent as he stood there,

silent now, before her. Then, when she nodded, he placed the record carefully on the machine and switched it on. She listened, transfixed, to the glorious voices of Flagstad and Melchior until Mark burst in to interrupt their climax. Harry rose, turned off the instrument, and faced her with a grave look of inquiry. Again she nodded, and he opened his kimono.

In the months that followed she found feverishly rewarding the different ways of lovemaking to which her imaginative and widely experienced guide introduced her. Their rendezvous were always in his apartment and took place at noon, on his ostensible lunch hour. In this new school she proved herself an eager and proficient student, and the guilt that now assailed her in every hour when she was not with him seemed even to add to the overall intensity of her pleasure. When she thought of the horror that some of her doings would arouse in Rod (whose suspicion she was careful not to arouse by any interruption of marital relations), or in her father; when she heard, ringing in her head, their imagined exclamations of "decadent" or "depraved," she thought, with an acceptance and resignation, that heaven and hell had to be different places, and never the twain should meet.

On Harry she now felt a dependence that was more like the blind devotion of a dog than a love in any romantic sense of the word. She took him as a kind of new god who had ravished her and become her master. One Sunday morning, when Rod was again away on a business trip, and she had gone to Harry's flat instead of taking the girls to church, and found herself nude, kneeling on his living room rug, her hands clasping his bare buttocks and her lips receiving his ejaculated sperm, she knew, with a dreary satisfaction, that she had no further to fall.

6

Saint Jude's, the Episcopal boys' boarding school to which the twelve-year-old Rod Jessup had been sent by his father, himself a devoted graduate, managed to imply to a visitor, in the gray Gothic architecture of its rather severe oblong campus, that a strict adherence was therein paid to the commandments handed down on Mount Sinai. And indeed the boys adhered to most of them, certainly to the most important. They found a single God more than enough, and had no call for any others; they never even thought of making graven images, and they could hardly fail to remember the Sabbath day, so heavily emphasized in their weekly schedule. They honored their parents, in their own way, and the ideas of murder, theft, adultery or false witness (whatever that was) never crossed their minds, nor did they covet their neighbor's wife or his servants or his ox or his ass. But they did covet a number of other things, and they certainly took the Lord's name in vain whenever out of hearing of the faculty. Such, however, had to be minor violations of the code, and there were no injunctions against smutty talk or masturbation or any of the little sex games that one boy may play with another when only boys are attainable for the sport. So life went on pleasantly enough under the irrelevant prattle of Sunday preachers and instructors in sacred studies. The boys knew well enough how little their families at home cared for these.

Rod, by the age of fourteen, was not only a very beautiful boy; he was a good student, an able athlete and an enthusiastic participant in all the major extracurricular school activities. He was a popular enough fellow, but he earned the hostility of some whose lewd invitations to bedtime visits after lights he rejected with scorn and contempt. It was not fatal to decline such bids, but the boys' etiquette outlawed any sermonizing, and Rod felt compelled to condemn what he deemed sinful. A group, accordingly, was organized to teach a lesson in humility to this "Christer." Six of them grabbed Rod when he was taking a shower in the gym and rushed him to a deserted corner of the locker room where they held him down on the floor and tickled his testicles and tweaked his penis until he ejaculated, at which point they fled, with hoots of laughter.

They all assumed that Rod would soon forget the matter. They even liked him and hoped that he would profit by the experience and be less of a prude in the future. But they were wrong. Rod did not forget it, nor did it in any way alter his moral stance against their ideas of sexual fun. It did, however, have one serious repercussion with him. He never sought personal retaliation against any of the six. He did not feel that he had the right to do so, because — though he would have gone to the stake rather than admit it — he now saw himself as one of them.

For there had been something deep within him that had not entirely rejected this initiation into shared sexual activity, something in the very intensity of his public humiliation, in the actual shame of it, that had been physically titillating. Horrors! But had he really struggled very hard to fight them off? No! For he might have done so; they were not so impassioned as to carry out their project at the risk of a really bloody fistfight, of which they all knew him capable. One of them, Harry Hammersly, the next day, had actually gripped Rod on the shoulder walking to chapel and murmured in his ear with a grin, "You didn't really mind it, did you, Rod? You know, if you want, you can do it to me any day!" And Rod hadn't killed him! He even allowed Harry to join his group on a bird watch the following Sunday afternoon.

But Rod's mood darkened in the following weeks. He began to shun even friendly groups and take long walks alone on weekend afternoons; he couldn't seem to live with this new image of a self afflicted with sensual yens. The boys who had played the trick on him began to be alarmed at what they had wrought: might this new Rod be so irresponsible as to expose them to the faculty? Even if their little trick was not to be found on Mount Sinai's list of don'ts, they knew only too well what a storm would be involved. But when they delegated Hammersly to intercede with Rod, he was given contemptuous assurance that no such exposure need be feared.

One spring vacation Rod was tempted to confide in his father. But Rodney Senior had suffered another heart attack and was resting at home, barred for some weeks from attending his office, and Rod's mother was very firm about his not being worried with anything. Yet the big, broadly smiling patient seemed to sense some of the boy's chagrin; he clapped a hand under his son's chin and made him look up into those serene gray eyes and hear the gentle paternal tone: "Rod, dear boy, if there's something on your mind, you should be able to tell your poor old dad. I don't care if it's something you find a bit unattractive. We all have stinky thoughts and nasty urges. Maybe one day I'll tell you about mine. Oh, you'd be surprised! Maybe even shocked. We're monsters, my boy. We're all monsters. But monsters can be a little bit less monstrous if they love each other, don't you think? The way you and I and Mummy feel about each other. Isn't that so? Well, think it over, and if I can be the tiniest help to you, let me know. What else am I here for, for goodness' sake, if it isn't to help out a fine son like you?"

Rod's heart ached with love for this benevolent easygoing sire, so inexplicably stricken with a malady that Rod knew from his mother's agonized anxiety was darkly menacing. He felt that his father was a kind of god of boundless mercy stretching out open arms to enfold him in everlasting bliss if he could only allow himself to rush into that embrace. But he could not bring himself to believe that his father — for all his talk of monsters — could really tolerate the idea that any boy who hoped to become a man could possibly have derived any pleasure from the revolting thing that had been done to him. Could he even imagine his father in such a position? Hell and damnation!

He returned to school without having availed himself of the paternal offer to tell all. Yet even that Rodney Senior had seemed to understand. He had been as merry as usual in seeing his son off on the train. But a week later Rod was called into the headmaster's study and gravely informed that another attack had ended his father's life.

Eleanor Jessup was largely responsible for her son's surviving this crisis without major mental damage. She was a tall bony plain, exceedingly intelligent and intellectual woman, with messy reddish hair, a high brow and large nose, who regarded as the miracle of her life that she should have attracted such a man as her husband and never doubted that all hope for her future happiness had died with him. But she was a Roman in her sense of duty. She saw life too clearly to imagine for a moment that her son could make up to her for what his father had been or that she could make up to him for what he had lost. But together they could carry on; together they could be worthy of her husband's faith in them. With an admirable minimum of words she put steel in Rod's heart.

And they did carry on. Rod at school recovered his balance and his popularity. His goal in life was now a simple and all-encompassing one. He would strive to replace his father in the world, an ideal rather than a possibility. Whatever cesspools lurked in the cavities of his mind, his heart could be pure.

For the rest of their time at Saint Jude's Harry Hammersly cultivated Rod's friendship with what he at least regarded as considerable success. Rod was now among the leaders of the school — he had become a prefect and stroked the varsity crew — and though Harry was renowned and even a bit feared as a wit and had achieved the merely secondary distinction in a sports-worshiping academy of being editor of the school magazine, he enjoyed nothing like the popularity of the boy to whose friendship he aspired. He had, at least at school, far more to gain from Rod than Rod from him.

Rod's attitude towards Harry was more complicated. He could never, of course, forget the episode of the locker room; its fixed spot in his mind was even the core of his relationship with his new intimate. He never referred to it, but he developed the notion that by locating it essentially in Harry and assuring himself by their companionship that it was *there* and not in Rod Jessup, that he somehow had it under a kind of control. Harry, in a way, was thus everything that Rod was *not*, and his very presence seemed to make it possible for Rod to keep it that way.

Which did not in the least mean that he could not become fond of Harry. The latter's cultivation of him was flattering, and Harry cut a considerable figure among the more sophisticated minority of their class, even venturing to flaunt an occasional defiance against the solid wall of the athletic lobby. At Yale, of course, the balance tipped more in Harry's favor; there were even those in their undergraduate circle who found the abrasively ironic Harry a more amusing companion than the more staid and literal Rod, but at law school Rod was again in the lead, his compulsive industry raising him to an editorship of the Law Journal, while Harry's preoccupation with society and women limited him to the good but not top grades that his lightning grasp of the material brought him even in the few hours he accorded it.

Eleanor Jessup did not like Harry and had no scruples about making her opinion known to her son. She and Rod shared a small apartment off Riverside Drive, and she spent long days teaching history at a private girls' school, but there were some important New Yorkers who remembered with affection and admiration her brilliant and early cut-off mate, and she dined out from time to time in fashionable circles where her dry humor and terse wit were appreciated.

"I must admit, Rod dear," she confessed to him one morning at breakfast after one of these social evenings, "that seeing your friend Harry's parents, as I did last night, fawning over Mrs. Neely Vanderbilt, may provide some excuse for his worldly streak. They say Harry's father is completely bust and doesn't even pay his bridge debts. But there they are, he and his wife, the two old dowdies, dressed to the gills with probably unpaid raiment, desperately cadging invitations to Palm Beach or the Caribbean. Ugh! It's sickening to watch them at it."

"Poor old Harry! But he knows they have nothing more to give him. He's on his own now. And, you must admit, he does pretty well."

"I hope you never lend him money, Rod."

"He always seems to have more than I have!"

"And I wonder where he gets it."

"You've never been fair to Harry, Ma."

But Rod was never entirely sure of Harry himself. And when Harry followed his lead successfully in applying for a job in Vollard Kaye, he began to see him as a potential rival. Fortunately they were assigned to different departments, Harry having elected trusts and estates where his charm and cozy manners with individual clients, particularly rich elderly ladies, were strong assets and where the hours were not as long as in other sections. Rod, of course, reveled in the corporate work which constituted the firm's main business. And when the year came for both to be made partners, and both were, Rod was reassured to know that there would be no further question as to which was the more qualified candidate for the future leadership of the firm. It would have to be a corporate man.

Relaxed on the subject of competition, Rod was now able to take an unmitigated pleasure in Harry's usually pleasant company. It was gratifying to see his friend rising to the top of a department that was a satisfactorily contributing part of the firm but not one that would ever be able to dominate management. For Rod still maintained secret doubts about Harry's innate sense of right and wrong and would not have cared to see him in a position where he could in any way alter the sacred tenets that maintained the firm's esprit de corps, tenets which, of course, had been laid down by Ambrose Vollard. But with his widows and young heirs and trusts Harry helped to run a lively department and kept the partners highly amused at the firm lunches with his merry tales of family frictions and extravagances. Oh yes, Vollard Kaye would always have a place for Harry.

And he amused Vinnie. That, alas, was becoming an important thing. Rod had been troubled that she did not seem to gain happiness with the years. She never complained, and always insisted impatiently that she was just fine, and for him not to be such a worrywart about her, but there it was: things were not as they should be for a woman of her looks and charm and general capability. And if Harry could take time off from his own busy social schedule to escort her to an occasional play or concert or opera, well, that was just fine, wasn't it?

7

ONE MORNING WHEN ROD had an uptown appointment, he decided after lunch not to go back to his office, but to spend the afternoon working in his apartment. The girls would be at school until five, and Vinnie had gone to Glenville for the day, so it would be quiet. He kept certain of his files in a closet that was also used as a liquor cabinet, and it was usually kept locked, as their cleaning woman was not above the temptation of an occasional nip. He had different hiding places for the key, and he now remembered that he had slipped it into one of the drawers of his wife's dressing table under a pile of her under- wear. Reaching for it, his hands struck a notebook. Flipping its pages in surprise, he saw it was full of Vinnie's handwriting, and after he had made out one sentence, he sat heavily down, ice sliding over his heart like a rapid glacier, and read the jour- nal through.

Vinnie had faithfully recorded what she and Harry had done. The journal was an inventory of their acts. What had in- duced her to record the shameful list? Some remnant of con- science, some throwback to her mother's puritan ancestry? For a wild moment he thought it might be fiction. But it was too graphic. For another his astonishment was so great that he could almost set aside the scarlet fact that his world was now in tiny pieces, scattered all over the room. When he rose at last to his feet, he tottered and almost fell. Then he returned the journal to its place and closed the drawer. He left the apartment and walked over to Central Park where he sat for an hour on a bench.

What he began to realize, slowly but with a creeping ineluctability, was that this experience, which was like nothing that had ever happened to him before, seemed to be occurring to a person other than himself, perhaps even an opposite. For what sort of man would have married a woman capable of doing what Vinnie had described on the last page of her abominably honest journal? Or did all women do it, or want to do it, and had he been living in a paradise of idiotic fools? Was it even conceivable that he would want a woman to do it to *him*? Was *that* why the horrid journal had an eerie fascination for him, over and above the wrath and indignation it inspired? How could he know what might or might not arouse the lust of the new man that Rod Jessup had become in a single morning?

He then walked rapidly around the reservoir, only to find that his head was aching, and there was a queer buzzing in his ears. He returned to his bench and sat there until this stopped. He then proceeded to face his problem with all the clarity his legal training had given him. Was there anything left of his life, and if so, what? There were his daughters, of course, but this did not directly affect them. And there was the firm. Ah yes, the firm and Ambrose Vollard. Above the general rubble of his hopes and purposes the figure of his father-in-law loomed like an isolated tower. And Ambrose *could* be directly affected! Faced with the low conduct of his idolized daughter, might he not be hit in the very heart of his idealistic nature? Might the disillusionment not spread to stain even the beautiful windows of the church of law that he had so lovingly constructed? His partner Harry cuckolding his partner Rod with his own child! Would *that* be the logo of Vollard Kaye?

No, that had to be avoided at all cost.

He rose, walked a hundred paces and returned to his bench. There was a way out. What Harry and Vinnie had done together and what they would presumably continue to do, could only be made right by one thing: their marriage. Their sin would be successfully encapsulated by a union sanctioned by law. It would even be legitimized, as were babes born before wedlock by the nuptials of their parents. That Vinnie would be more than willing to wed her paramour he had no doubt from the ecstasies of her journal. And that Harry would consent to become the son-in-law of the senior partner . . . ! Rod's cynical shrug expressed his new opinion of his erstwhile friend. Ambrose Vollard need never know to what depths his beloved daughter had sunk. He would only have to face the fact, common enough among his acquaintance, that she had married twice.

So he had only to dispose of himself to save both Ambrose and his firm. Suicide? Hardly. A search for his motive might follow, and heaven only knew what clues would be picked up. No, Rodman Jessup had to be removed from the picture by a method that would cast no shadow on any but himself. And there was really only one way to accomplish *that*.

He left the park and called his secretary from a booth to tell her to inform his wife that he had been called suddenly out of town on business. And the secretary was to go to his apartment and pack a suitcase of his clothes and bring it to his club. All-efficient, she would do this well. Then he called a friend of Harry's who was also a somewhat lesser one of his and Vinnie's: Lila Fisk. Was she free by any chance to dine with him at the Colony Restaurant? She was a bit surprised, but yes, she was free, and a few hours later he faced her across a corner table at the costliest eatery in town, raising his cocktail glass to click it against hers in a silent toast.

Raven-haired, alabaster pale, with a conspiratorial smile, rich and richly attired in black satin with large pearls, Lila Fisk was a plump but still radiant forty. She was also a hearty and genial divorcée who had been wed three times and had apparently retired from the matrimonial market to live entirely for pleasure. She was a great pal of Harry Hammersly's, through whom she had come to know the Jessups. Vinnie, who was not usually partial to epicurean types, had recently taken to her. It was not hard now for Rod to understand why. Were they not sisters under the skin? He was also sufficiently aware that Lila found him physically attractive. He was not so unsophisticated as to be ignorant of the fact that a virtuous man was apt to act as a challenge to a woman like her.

"Are you having a row with Vinnie?" she demanded.

"Why do you ask?"

"You're not a man to ask a lady out without your wife unless you have a point to make. You want to get back at her for something."

"It couldn't be because the man finds himself greatly attracted to the lady?"

"Oh, it could be. But then he'd take her to a less conspicuous spot. That's Arlina, the gossip columnist, over there. And don't think she hasn't already taken us in."

"Do you care?"

"I don't give a damn. But I want you to know what I know. And now let's not spoil our evening with too many questions."

They talked, merrily enough, on other topics — she was an omnivorous reader, an avid theater goer and a baseball fan — and after dinner they went to her handsome Park Avenue apartment, where, after several drinks, they made what is sometimes called love. He was surprised how simple she made it and that it was not followed, in his case, by the least feeling of guilt. Yet she wouldn't let him spend the night; she kicked him out at midnight, with the injunction, "If you want to make it up with Vinnie now, you'll find it easier. Revenge will have cooled your anger."

But the last thing he was going to do was make anything up with Vinnie. He dressed and went to his club. How much, he wondered, did Lila know about Harry and Vinnie? He didn't care enough, anyway, to ask her. She agreed to dine out with him twice more, including a visit to a nightclub where they were photographed together, but when he suggested that he move from his club into her apartment, she was profoundly shocked.

"Are you out of your mind? Nobody today objects to an affair, if it's carried on with some discretion, but women my age don't *live* with men. Not in society, anyway. Not yet. Are you trying to ruin what shred of reputation I have left?"

"What's wrong with our living together?"

"What's wrong? What's right! Do you want to drive Vinnie into divorcing you for adultery? Oh, my God, maybe that's just what you *do* want! You're a lunatic, Rodman Jessup! Go home to your club, or wherever you hang out, and don't come near me again until you've learned to act like a gentleman!"

The unusual thing about the next three months was that not once, even through the divorce proceedings and the negotiations following his resignation from the firm, did Rod have a word of direct communication with his wife or her father or Harry Hammersly. It took firmness on his part, but he arranged it. Vollard Kaye always sent a neutral partner to deal with him.

8

SOME WEEKS AFTER Harry Hammersly's interview with Ambrose Vollard and their decision to sue Rodney in New York, Harry sat in his office, the door closed, contrary to the usual Vollard Kaye policy, having told his pretty secretary, Miss Peltz, that he would take no calls before his meeting with Jack Owens, the young partner who would be doing the legwork in the Jessup case. He had spent a good part of such little spare time as he had, musing about the matter. What the devil had brought about such a revolution in the conduct, and apparently in the character, of Vinnie's husband? Could he have discovered her affair? But in that case why would he ape her and not denounce her? And jettison his whole law career into the bargain? And alienate her father, whom he had always professed to adore? It couldn't be passion, for no man, not even one as naïve as Rod, could feel passion for so easy a lay as Lila Fisk. And besides, Owens had reported that he wasn't seeing her now.

Harry's eyes roamed restlessly over the vivid decorations of his chamber: the Toulouse-Lautrec poster of Yvette Guilbert, the Mucha one of Sarah Bernhardt as Lorenzaccio, the varnished mahogany bookcase with its gleamingly new law reports, the Persian carpet and the marble-topped Renaissance table-desk with its silver appointments in parallel rows, devoid of papers or other clutter, his way of presenting a client with the stripped cleanness of his total attention. How different from the mess of files and printed drafts that covered Rod's desk, stacked around large photographs of his daughters hugging spaniels!

Had he always resented Rod? Was it because he had once liked him too much? But surely one could overemphasize such things. Yes, he had such a thing about Rod at age fourteen — wasn't that a typical stage in a boy's sexual development? Look at the English public schools, for Pete's sake! When those Brits grew up they married and conquered the world. And hadn't he and Rod become the best of friends after his own tastes had turned to the other sex? Yes, but. But what? Why was he always cursed with this habit of being honest with himself? Yet there it was, his jealousy of Rod's looks, Rod's boasted ethics, Rod's so-called knight-errantry and his easy success with everything and everybody. Was all *that* the real reason behind his delight in being sucked off by Rod's wife?

But that would only be if he had wanted Rod to know. And he hadn't; he had taken the greatest precautions that Rod shouldn't know. And he wasn't the sort of man who would seduce a woman solely to satisfy an injured ego; he cared about Vinnie and giving her a fuller life. He might have been a bit of a shit, but he was also the good guy that many people liked and esteemed. He hadn't wanted to break up a marriage. On the contrary, he had been all for the status quo. He had wanted everyone to go on as they were.

No, it was Rod who had broken things up. It was Rod who had left the firm. And if he had left a vacancy both in the firm and in the senior partner's family that Harry Hammersly could properly and legitimately fill, would it not be folly and arrant sentimentality for Harry Hammersly not to step forward and play his hand in every way that his trumps and honors could win? Wasn't Rod, for that matter, as much of a shit himself? He and his Lila Fisk! Ugh!

His telephone purred. "I'm sorry, Mr. Hammersly, but your mother's on the phone. She says it's important."

"Yes, Ma?" he barked into the instrument.

"Darling, you know that Boston trust I told you about? The one where the income is just piled up and might make your friend Vinnie rich one day? Well, I've just heard, from an impeccable Boston source, my cousin Lily Cole, that the second and final measuring life — if that's what you call it — old Mrs. Foxy Harrison, has just had another bad stroke."

"Ma! I hope you didn't bring me into your discussion. In any way!"

"Of course not. You can trust your old mater."

Which he was not about to do, though Gwendolyn Hammersly could be a valuable informant. She had long been anxious to see her only child and son married, but well married, and she had first regarded Vinnie, of whose affair with him she was cognizant, as an impediment. But with the prospect of Vinnie's being freed from wedlock she had turned her realistic attention to the latter's qualifications as a bride for what seemed a fatally attracted son, and she was coming to the conclusion that they were not so bad.

SHE AND PIERRE, Harry's father, had burst in on Harry on the very evening of the day when the news broke about Rod's escapade. They had been dressed as usual in all their finery for one of their ceaseless evening engagements, but had made time to stop by his apartment for a cocktail, which in the paternal case was always more than one.

"I was never so surprised in my life!" his mother had exclaimed. "I thought that shoe was on the other foot, if you know what I mean."

"Mother, hush up! Please!"

"What's wrong?" She glanced towards the bedroom door. "Have you got someone hidden in there, you naughty boy?"

There was nothing Harry could do about his parents. There never had been. Not young when they had married and produced him, they were still possessed of outstanding looks, he, gray and straight and slick, she, blond and slim and willowy, both attired as only the rich should be. As was often said about them, "The one thing you can't believe is that they have no money." Of old but impoverished families, it had been assumed by the New York society of 1915 that they would trade their beauty and lineage at the altar for fortunes, but when instead they joined their poverties and he became a war hero in the Lafayette Escadrille, they were for a time a romantic legend. Alas, this had hardly survived the ensuing decades of gambling, borrowing and drinking, in his case, and in hers the dubious chaperonage of indiscreet debutantes, the cadging of weekend invitations and the sponsorship of inferior beauty aids.

Yet some of it, miraculously, had. There were still those, if a diminishing number, who stood by the "charming Hammerslys." And Harry was smart enough to perceive that if everybody knew about his parents, his parents still *knew* everybody. And they could still do something for him.

And he loved them, too, in his own way. He even helped them out financially from time to time, but only when things were really desperate. He knew there was no changing their ways.

"And how is dear Vinnie taking this?" his mother had asked. Her tone was so solicitous that one might have thought she really cared. Vinnie had seen Gwendolyn Hammersly on many occasions with Harry, and, as Harry well knew, thoroughly disliked her, but Gwendolyn was little concerned with likes and dislikes. The world was a stage, and people acted their little parts. "Is it true there's going to be a divorce, right here in New York?"

"Why ask me, Ma? Haven't you checked out all the facts?"

"And it's so, then, that you're handling the case?"

"Better watch your step, my boy." This came from Pierre Hammersly, nursing a dark drink by the window from which he gazed vacantly over Harry's yard. "Representing a lovely lady in distress may lead to deeper commitments. Otis Sterne married Mrs. Hoops after getting her divorce from Jim. Same thing happened with the Ulricks."

"Was that such a bad thing?" Harry inquired.

"Well, it's true that the lawyer in each case got his ass in a tub of butter."

"Pierre, your language!"

"Oh, come off it, Gwen. I've heard you use that expression."

"But not before our dear boy here." She turned to Harry. "Your father does have a point, anyway. When such a good friend of yours as Vinnie becomes free, there's bound to be speculation as to what you two will do about it. Now don't interrupt, darling, I'm just speculating. You will, of course, do just what you want. You always have, and it's stood you, on the whole, in good stead. All I'm doing is trying to make the picture clear to you. And I think I can supply a few facts that will interest you. All right?"

Harry had nodded. He knew what a gossip she was, but he also knew that she rarely spoke without a basis of fact. Her chatter on occasion could rise to the level of military intelligence.

"We have to give some thought as to what Vinnie's expectations are," his mother began. "I know she has something of her own that her parents have settled on her."

"Oh yes. But it's no fortune." Harry laughed. "Dr. Johnson said of a dinner that it was well enough but not one to ask a man to. Vinnie's fortune is hardly one to marry for."

"And I suppose her father will leave her something."

"Don't count too much on that." Pierre now came from the window to add his bit to the discussion. "It's not like the old days when lawyers like William Nelson Cromwell and Francis Stetson were paid in clients' stock and made fortunes. But I daresay Mrs. Vollard will cut up well. Those Bostonians always have more than you think."

"But she has too many children, Pierre. Now listen to me, both of you. There's something you don't know, either of you. I learned about it today, from Lily Cole. Have you heard about the Waldo trust?" Her listeners shook their heads. "Well, it was set up by a crazy old bachelor great-uncle of Mrs. Vollard's who hated everybody in his family but had hopes for their posterity. He measured it by the two youngest lives among his nephews and nieces and provided that the income should be accumulated. It has been invested and reinvested for decades and has apparently reached a fabulous figure. When it breaks, which can't be too far off now, it gets divided among a host of relatives, but it's still so big that Vinnie's share should be a couple of million!"

Harry had listened to her carefully. He knew that such a trust was quite possible under Massachusetts law, and the eccentricity of the scheme fitted well with many Boston legends.

"Thank you, Ma. And now maybe you'd better be getting on to your party."

He didn't have to tell her how interested he was. She was

only too well aware of that. They were indeed birds of a feather. The next day he had telephoned a friend in a Boston firm and asked him about the Waldo trust. The friend did not know all the details but he confirmed its existence and the general knowledge that many Waldos and Shattucks and Lowells expected to be one day enriched by it. That was all Harry needed to know. To seek to know more might seem too calculating — even to himself.

For he was genuinely fond of Vinnie. How could he not be? She had made him an amusing, compliant and sexually satisfying mistress. Why should she not make him an equally good wife? Would it hurt that she should also provide wealth and social advantage? Wasn't it in everybody's best interest? Wasn't it in *hers*? Was she, an abandoned wife and perhaps herself the subject of detrimental anecdotes, in any position to expect a better match than himself, the amusing, the popular, the brilliant Harry Hammersly? For that, laugh who may, was what he was!

Miss peltz called again; Jack Owens was there, a very grave and dedicated young lawyer, the youngest indeed of the partners, and chosen by Harry for this case as the one who knew Rod the least.

"I've been to see Jessup at his club," he told Harry. "And very cooperative I found him. He insists that he will represent himself in any proceedings we take, and that he will offer no defense to a charge of adultery. He, of course, wishes to know what property demands we will make of him."

"Did he say anything about his job prospects?"

"Only that he's had a couple of offers already."

"I don't doubt that."

"And that he hopes to be able to contribute substantially to the support of his two daughters."

"He will have every opportunity."

"And he hopes to have the usual visitation rights with the children."

"No trouble about that. We have no complaints about him as a father."

Owens looked faintly surprised. "Even considering the company he's keeping?"

"We understand he's not keeping any company."

"Does that mean we should work for a reconciliation?"

"In no way."

"Then there's only left the question of alimony."

"Mrs. Jessup will take no alimony."

Owens frowned and paused a moment before asking, "Shouldn't we be a bit afraid of that?"

"Afraid? Why?"

"That will look . . . some people might say anyway . . . that she gave him cause for what he did?"

Harry tightened his lips. How much did Owens know? Did the whole office know? Miss Peltz, he knew, was a great gossip, and she might well have smelled him out. And then there was always his dear Mama! But he reminded himself that what people heard or thought they heard didn't really matter, for they always made up their own minds on what they chose to believe, and one could do little to alter their conclusions, true or false. One just had to keep going on what at least *looked* like a consistent track.

"I don't think Mrs. Jessup gives a damn how it may look or what people will say," Harry retorted at last. "She won't take anything for herself. So draft me up something about the children, the usual weekend and summer provisions — take the

Bennett agreement for a model — and leave blank the spaces for child support payments, and I'll go over it with her."

When Owens had left, Miss Peltz called him to tell him that Mrs. Jessup herself had arrived and was waiting to see him. As soon as Vinnie was seated at his desk before him, and the door reclosed, he told her of Owens's objection.

"It's just what I warned you about, Vinnie. It won't look well for you to skip the alimony. If you don't want it yourself, why not take it and put it in trust for the children?"

"Never!" she exclaimed, in a spurt of sudden temper. "Take money from poor Rod? After what you and I have been doing! Why, it would be shameless!"

"But, Vinnie —"

"No, Harry, no! I'm speaking to my lawyer now, not my lover, and I expect to be obeyed. Unless you want me to get another. Lawyer, I mean."

There was something distinctly different about Vinnie that morning. Or perhaps something reminiscent of how she had been before their intimate relations. As his mistress she had appeared to entertain for him an almost cowering devotion, totally unlike the rather mocking friendliness that had preceded it. He had privately relished the supposition that he had given her the thrill and satisfaction that she had not found with her less imaginative spouse. Whatever it was, however, it was now in eclipse. The old Lavinia was more than apparent in her tone.

She took his silence as assent to her alimony decision, and went on: "There's something else it behooves you to know, Harry. Certainly as my lawyer, anyway. Something I've just found out myself."

Harry eyed her intently. Was she going to tell him she didn't love him? "Something about yourself?"

"Oh, very much about myself. I'm pregnant."

"Vinnie!" He jumped to his feet. Then, as quickly, he re-seated himself. "But that's wonderful news!"

Her stare was blank. "Why wonderful?"

His brain seemed to whirl. One of his doubts about marriage was whether she could have a child; none had followed the birth of her younger daughter. He hadn't been sure how much he really wanted one, but now he *knew*! He wanted one very much! "Because it will be our child, darling, yours and mine. We'll marry and love it and bring it up together . . . Oh, it will all be fine!"

"Aren't you taking a lot of things for granted? Me, to begin with. And secondly, the 'ourness' of the child?"

"You mean it's not ours?"

"Oh, it's mine, all right. But there may be a question if it's yours. I had not discontinued sexual relations with Rod. And what he and I did together was rather more child producing than *some* of the things you and I did."

Could a fetus in a womb make two women out of one? Harry felt chilled before this new Vinnie. But not jealous. Not, oddly enough, the least jealous.

"You never told me you were still sleeping with Rod."

"Why should I have? It was my business, and my business alone, how best to handle a husband in such a situation. I didn't want to deny him anything that might arouse his suspicions. And we didn't take any precautions, any more than you and I did, believing, as I did, what the doctor told me after my sec-ond daughter was born. Well, he was wrong. Obviously, I *could* have another child."

Harry was almost surprised himself at his now impetuous offer. "But Rod's child or mine, I'll be his father if you'll marry me!"

"His? You assume it will be a boy?"

"I do."

"Why, for God's sake?"

"Because you're like Lady Macbeth today. 'Bring forth men children only!'"

"But she hadn't already produced two daughters."

"By Rod!"

"I see. And not by you." She nodded slowly. "Well, the news seems to have done strange things to you. And I will admit I think you're behaving rather well. So how about this. We'll go ahead with the divorce as planned. Rod seems bent on that. And as for you and me, we'll wait until the child is born. If it's yours I'll marry you."

He gaped. "But how will you know?"

"Oh, I'll know. Mothers always do."

"That's an old wives' tale, Vinnie!"

"Well, then, I'm an old wife."

WHEN JACK OWENS reported to Rod Jessup, as Harry supposed they had to, that Vinnie was pregnant, Rod at once waived all rights to the unborn infant. This amounted to a voucher that the child was none of his, and Harry impressed upon Owens the importance of not revealing it to anyone in the firm, particularly to Ambrose Vollard. He sought, unsuccessfully he could only suppose, to convince the young man that Jessup's attitude betrayed an hysterical jealousy by the need to excuse his own infidelity.

Five months later Vinnie gave birth to a fine healthy son.

Almost at the same time, the Boston great-aunt died, and the Waldo trust should have terminated. But it didn't. Harry had the mortification of reading in a Boston journal that Waldo had used as a measure the old common-law maximum limitation of two lives in being plus twenty-one years. The two lives were no longer in being, but the period in gross of a legal majority was just beginning! For all his bitterness Harry still found occasion for an ironic guffaw at his own incapacity. How could he have forgotten a limitation that he had learned in his first year at law school?

The first evening that he was allowed to call upon Vinnie, now Mrs. Vollard Jessup as her divorce caused her to be named, she led him into the baby's room and asked the nurse to leave them. Together they looked down at the bawling child.

"You see he wants a father," Vinnie announced with a smile. "And I have every intention of giving him one."

"But whom?"

"You're the lucky man."

"How do you know?"

"Look at him, silly."

Indeed, the cleft chin and the slight hook of the nose were models of Harry's own. But, even more than that, he felt a sudden conviction that she was right, and he was seized by a totally novel exaltation.

"He's mine!" he cried.

She laughed. "And mine, too, I hope."

"Yes, you'll have to marry me now!"

"Just for his sake?"

"Isn't that enough?"

She looked away with a slight shrug. "I guess it will have to be."

He did not turn to her. His eyes were fixed on the child, who had stopped crying and seemed to be staring at him. "It's all right, sonny," his lips silently articulated. "I'll give you the world." It even crossed his mind that the boy would have just attained his majority when his mother would come into her share of the Waldo trust. The child's father would see to it that she made a proper settlement on the young man.

9

❦

THE NEXT FIVE YEARS marked the rise to local glory of Harry Hammersly. Married to Lavinia and son-in-law of the senior partner, he took over Rod Jessup's old position of heir apparent, at least in the eyes of the younger partners, now a majority. Heir presumptive, in Harry's own private opinion, might have been the more accurate term. For Ambrose bore nothing like the same affection for this second son-in-law that he had borne for the first. It was true that he respected Harry's undoubted legal abilities, and found him particularly valuable in taking off his burdened shoulders some of the trickier problems of management. But he could never feel that Harry was really with him in what he deemed the most vital function of his own professional life: the tight welding together of a group of profound and idealistic legal minds in a unit of mutual respect and affection. He more than suspected that Harry's eye was fastened, perhaps to the exclusion of other considerations, on the annual figure of the firm's net profits.

And he was right. Harry read the future very differently from the way his wife's father read it. He saw size as the name of the future game, and the greatest prizes going to the biggest firms. He understood perfectly that Vollard Kaye was considered a jewel case among the firms representing major corporations and that its list of clients was the envy of downtown, but he also saw that by expanding its business into the areas of celebrity divorces, family feuds in Gotham, stockholders' strike suits, deadly proxy battles, medical malpractice and other fields of legal combat openly sniffed at by the ethically snobbish Ambrose, he could double the size of the firm and more than double its net profits. He was already having quiet lunches with Morris Applebaum, of Applebaum, Levy & Knox, who enjoyed a brilliant practice in all the areas shunned by Vollard Kaye, but who lacked a strong corporate department. A merger with them, in Harry's eyes, would be a merger made in heaven, though it was only too clear that in Ambrose's far from silent view, it would be made in the other place.

For such a union would involve the taking in of some twenty-five new partners and placing them above Vollard Kaye associates who had been led to believe that they had no rivals in ascending the firm ladder other than those hired originally out of law school like themselves. The joined firms would constitute a unit markedly different from the present Vollard Kaye, for Ambrose's particular variety of esprit de corps would be bound to be lost in sheer numbers and with partners not trained in his philosophy. Harry recognized that Vollard, Applebaum & Hammersly (for his imagination had already placed his name in the new firm) would have lost the unique reputation its predecessor now enjoyed in the legal world, but he was sure that this loss would be compensated, at least in the eyes of the younger partners, by a "gross" that would put it among the first firms in the nation!

Nor did he have any serious qualms about working in a kind of underground against his father-in-law's principles. He saw the future as ineluctable and Ambrose's idealistic concept of a law firm as a quaint relic of a picturesque but disappearing past.

To oppose the big black curling breakers of the coming sea was as futile and even ludicrous as leading knights of the round table into the surging foam. Their very armor would pull them down. Sad, but was it Harry's fault if Ambrose chose the role of Don Quixote? While he Harry, the supreme surfer, would slide to glory on the crest of the beetling wave?

And he had more now than just himself to think about. He had his son, or "stepson" as the world was asked to believe, young Ambrose Jessup, a fine, healthy little lad, almost comically resembling him, who had the sense already to show a marked preference for his jovial, gift-bearing, fun-sharing "stepfather" over his more remote and often preoccupied mother. Young Ambrose might ultimately rise to take the place of his maternal grandfather and namesake in the family firm (a firm to which his "stepfather" would have ultimately made the greater contribution), but if the boy chose another career, well, Harry would see that he had the best start in that!

One thing that seemed to bode well for Harry's projected merger was a marked decline in old Ambrose's mental and physical health. He had always been subject to periodic spells of depression, but ever since Rod Jessup had quit the firm, they had become more frequent and more prolonged. The staff had gradually fallen into the habit of referring all administrative questions to Harry. Vacuums are soon filled. And one of such questions was that of moving the firm from its old quarters, which it had long occupied in a superannuated building on Wall Street, to a new gleaming glass cube with a breathtaking view of the harbor. There was also plenty of available space in the structure to accommodate the Applebaum firm should the merger ever be effected.

Ambrose, reluctantly accompanying his son-in-law on an inspection tour of the proposed site, grumbled a bit as they traversed the empty white corridors and empty white chambers. "It's all very swell, of course, Harry. A bit too swell, if you ask me, which I'm not entirely sure you're planning to. I can never forget how, in my uncle's old offices, he used to remind people, if they couldn't find a document in the safe, to look underneath it, for there was a hole in its bottom. That was the kind of relaxed, genteel atmosphere I cherished! Can't imagine it happening here."

Harry smiled in a show of sympathy. He had heard the story many times before. They were nearing the end of their visit, and he now guided his senior's footsteps to a vast corner office whose four large windows framed the dramatic panorama of Governor's Island and the Statue of Liberty.

"And for what monarch will this be the throne room?" Ambrose growled.

"Need you ask, sir?"

The older man was touched, in spite of himself. Even he could be dazzled. He gave Harry a little cuff on the shoulder.

"Get thee behind me, Satan!"

Vinnie had watched the rising tension between her father and husband with apprehension. She had not lost her high post in the paternal affections, but she was no longer the intimate confidante she had once been. Ambrose seemed to be retiring further and further into himself. And it was she who needed him now, as he had once needed her. Being Harry's wife, she found, was a very different thing from being his mistress.

Was it marriage that had changed Harry? Or paternity? Or simply the elimination of Rod between himself and his goal in the firm? In any case, he was a much more serious person. Harry had still his old biting and sarcastic humor, but it was tempered now with a new habit of mild frowns, and his old shrill laugh had been muted to a rather smug chuckle. He had become somehow more focused, but on what she was not sure, except that it was certainly not his wife.

They had at last one of those discussions that suddenly erupt into irate recognitions of differences that each has known were long smoldering in the other.

"I wish you'd go a little easier on Dad," she had begun and then faltered, for he had looked immediately and sharply up. "I mean about this new office and all. You know how he hates changes. But time will maybe do a lot, if you'll just be patient."

"Time is something we don't have an infinite amount of, my dear. Its very name implies it. And markets have to be taken advantage of. Real estate markets, especially."

"But you don't want to hurt him, do you?"

"I don't *want* to, of course not. But men who stand pat before the juggernaut of the future must expect to be pushed aside."

"My father, Harry, is not a man to be pushed aside."

"Then let him stand gracefully out of the way."

This angered her. "You seem to have this fixed idea that the future belongs to you. I don't see any reason for such pessimism. Why shouldn't it belong equally well to Daddy? He's certainly done more than you have to make the present what it is."

"You will oblige me, Lavinia, by not talking about things you know nothing about."

"Why should I give a damn about obliging you?" Vinnie's voice was rising. "And I *do* know what I'm talking about! I'm talking about human decency and plain ordinary gratitude!"

"How does gratitude come into it?"

"How can you ask? Anyway, I'll tell you! Gratitude for all my father has done for you. He has simply made you, and you know it. Yes, he and I, too. Where the hell do you think Harry Hammersly would be without the two of us?"

"Just about where he is today," Harry responded coolly. "You don't understand these things. You never have, and I daresay you never will. You were raised to worship your father as a god. Well, he's still a mortal. He's been a clever lawyer who's constructed a highly competent firm — for its day. But that day is passing. He knows it, but he won't face it. That's why he's fortunate to have me to do it for him. In another firm he might, like Akele in *The Jungle Book*, have to fight a successor wolf to the death. With me, instead of a torn throat, he can look forward to a dignified and respected retirement."

Vinnie gazed at him, almost now in fear. "All I was suggesting was that you might go a bit slower with him," she muttered.

"I shall proceed at my own speed," was his inexorable reply. "The pace will be dictated by events and certainly not by any undue sentimentality. And while we're on the subject of your father there is something that I want *you* to take up with him. Something that I've given a lot of thought to. And it's something of which you may be a better proponent than I."

"And that is?"

"Young Ambrose is now five and has not been baptized. I want it done, and I want his name changed to Ambrose Hammersly."

"Oh no! What will people say?"

"I don't give a hoot in hell what people say. No doubt, some of them have said it already. I want my child to bear my name. I more than want it. I insist on it!"

"But Daddy has always assumed he's Rod's child! What difference does a name make? A stepson is just as good as a son, particularly when Rod never even sees the child. For heaven's sake, Harry, leave well enough alone!"

"What's the big deal? Why all the fuss?"

"Because if Daddy ever suspects that it wasn't his dear Rod

that caused the big stink but actually his darling daughter, he'll have a fit!"

"But you wouldn't have to tell him the truth."

"He can put two and two together. No, I can't do it. I can't be the one to tell him he threw his adored protégé out of the firm for something he hadn't done."

"What do you mean, hadn't done? Do you think he and Lila Fisk were playing tiddlywinks?"

"Hadn't done what Daddy couldn't forgive: being unfaithful to *me*. Lila Fisk was nothing, and you know it."

"Very well. If you won't go to your father, I will."

"But you won't tell him?"

"About us? I shall simply tell him that I cannot undertake the raising of his grandson unless the boy bears my name."

Vinnie knew she was licked.

Harry decided to challenge his father-in-law about the Applebaum merger at Ambrose's seemingly strongest post. This was at the biweekly partners' lunch, held in a private dining room at the Downtown Association, which old Ambrose regarded as the forum where he could still most effectively exercise his supposed leadership of the firm. There, entrenched behind the double crystalline martini that a waiter brought him immediately upon his appearance, dressed and seated as inconspicuously as any at the table, he gave the affable appearance of being just another member of the group he dominated. He would laugh heartily at the most banal joke of the least amusing partner, and give his total attention to the idlest administrative suggestion of the youngest and most earnest. At least in the past he had known just how to dispose lightly of a silly or divisive topic without offending its proponent, and how to rally the table into an amicable union when he was backed by only a few. He knew his partners were too smart not to know when they were being handled, but he also knew that they were flattered by the fact that it took a great artist to handle them.

Harry, on the day of his planned coup d'état, had taken advantage of the senior partner's belated appearance at the lunch table to tell an amusing but mildly uncomplimentary anecdote about him.

"You know, gentlemen, that I represent you at a monthly meeting of the administrative officers of the major downtown law firms where we discuss common problems of management. I was asked at the last one how we handled aging partners who were reluctant to see their percentages of profit cut. 'Oh,' I told them, 'Ambrose handles all that. And to the queen's taste. He takes the old boy out for lunch and tells him in the friendliest fashion, Look, Tom or Bill or whatever his name is, the time has come for us old farts to move over.' The old geezer is willing enough to go along with the boss, but when the smoke clears, he finds that only one old fart has moved over."

The general laughter that ensued subsided as Ambrose entered the chamber and took his seat.

"I paused in the doorway before coming in," he observed to all, with a wry smile. "I did not wish to interrupt Harry's story. I know it's often told about me, and, of course, there's not a word of truth in it. That's fame, I suppose. But to be serious for a moment, I might point out that our Harry's concern these days seems to be more with increases than cuts in partners' percentages. Some of you may have learned through the grapevine, as I have, that he's been flirting with Morris Applebaum. Tell us, Harry, what we should have to pay Morris and his partners if we took them in, as you seem to favor."

Harry wondered for a few seconds who might have betrayed him. Vinnie? He glanced around the table. But *any* of them might have! Didn't he know the world? And wasn't he ready for it? "Probably more than any of us are now making, sir," he replied boldly. "The merger would more than double our gross. Every one of us would be making substantially more money."

"And money is all we care about?"

Harry would have liked to have retorted that not all of the partners were wed to Boston heiresses, but he knew better. "I don't say that, sir, but we should always be on the lookout for new sources of income." He addressed himself now to the table. "Even the most profitable law practice is at risk these days. None of the firms have big capital, and a couple of bad years can break them. A single change in the tax law could wipe out a whole field of clients: say, the repeal of the exemption of municipal bonds. We hear a lot of chatter these days about how the world is growing too materialistic. It's not the case! It's the inflation of everything, particularly wages, that drives us to make more and more money. What choice do we have? Take the opera, for example. In Ambrose's youth, the so-called golden age, you could hire a man for a buck a night to carry a pike in the grand march of *Aïda*. Now you probably have to pay for his health insurance! We wanted a world where every man could earn a living wage. Well, we've got it! And one way or another we've got to pay for it. With associates' salaries going up and up, to say nothing of rent and malpractice insurance, we have to keep a constant eye on our books to see how we're doing. The question used to be: Did we have a good year? Already we're talking about: Did we have a good month? We may get to the point where we ask: Did we have a good day?"

"So Morris Applebaum and you, Harry," Ambrose retorted with heavy sarcasm, "do not, after all, have your ears pricked for the clink of gold pieces. You are simply engaged in a gallant struggle for survival in a society rotted by a rabid socialism?"

"All I'm saying, sir, is that the golden age of law practice, as I've heard you call it, like the golden age of opera, was at least as materialistic as our own. Because its seeming generosity and high ideals were based on the economic servitude of the majority."

"Out of which mire Morris Applebaum will lead us!" Ambrose cast a mocking eye around the table, as if to assess how many were with him. More than half? It was close. But enough for him to proceed as he had commenced. "Well, let me trust to the contrary. When the time comes for us to haul down our colors and hoist new ones, let me hope that they may not be his under which we shall march. Not under his sleazy divorce mill where cocktail waitresses wed to senile tycoons strip families of their inheritances! Or where ancient companies are looted and their faithful staffs fired by proxy pirates! Or where tax frauds are lauded for their ingenuity and embezzlers pardoned by bought politicians!"

Harry threw up his hands and laughed. "Objection, your honor," he cried. "I can only agree that such a practice would hardly benefit us. But who is offering it?"

"You are, sir!" Ambrose thundered, and the table was shocked into a continued silence. But he saw fit to soften his expression as he glanced around the table. He was not so far gone as not to see when the issue was close. "Enough of this, anyway. I think we should now discuss the choice of a country club for our spring office outing. I'm told that Piping Rock is taken for the day we wanted . . ."

But Harry was not about to lose what he saw was an advantageous moment to play his trump card. It was not a coincidence that he had sent the one Jewish partner out of town on a business trip to avoid the embarrassment of the discussion on which he was about to embark.

"Country clubs are indeed relevant to the subject I wish to bring up, Mr. V," he called loudly down the table. "For some of our earnest young associates have already expressed their hope to me that we will not patronize one guilty of racial and religious discrimination. These things are becoming very important today. And that is why I have the nerve to ask our senior partner if some of his objection to the Applebaum firm does not stem from the fact that a good half of their partners are Jewish?"

Ambrose looked as if the question was beneath contempt, but he soon took in the fact that his partners were looking to him for an answer without in the least finding the query out of order.

"My objection is not based on that, no sir," he retorted icily.

"But forgive me, Mr. V, if I point out that under your guidance and that of your distinguished uncle before you, the firm has become known in the law schools as not overfriendly to Jewish applicants. Is it entirely unfair that this has been attributed to us as a policy? In a city whose economic and cultural life is largely dominated by Jews we have exactly three. Two associates, who very likely will not be made partners, and one member of the firm, relegated to our smallest department, real estate. Surely this is not a coincidence."

"And you know damn well it's not, Harry. What are you getting at? That I'm anti-Semitic? Nonsense! I have the greatest liking and respect for the considerable number of my Jewish friends. But when you're putting together an institution of a certain type of manners and morals, it makes sense to go in for a certain quantity of homogeneity. The particular trademark of Vollard Kaye is an old Yankee tradition of integrity, courage and gentlemanly behavior. Indeed, you can't mistake it. Now I'm not saying for a minute that Jews and Moslems and Chinamen and blacks are lacking in any of these virtues, but it so happens that they put them together in a different showcase."

"And that's not the showcase you want?"

"Well, let's simply put it that it's not *my* showcase. Is that anti-Semitism?"

"You know, I rather think it is. Or at least that there are people who would call it that."

Ambrose had turned pink. "Hammersly, you have been a disruptive influence in the firm ever since Rod left us! But I'll have you know I'm not going to sit idly by while you use your specious arguments to tear down the firm I've spent a lifetime putting together!"

Harry saw that he had lost that round, but he had expected to lose it, and he had not lost much. He was fairly confident that the younger partners were in favor of his projects; the future was almost inevitably his. What he had to do now was work on the wavering members, individually. He did this over an extended period of time, at lunches for two, always premised initially on another topic to be discussed and then gradually converted to his opportunity to make disclosures about Ambrose.

"You know, of course, there's not a man in the world for whom I have a greater affection or respect. But that can't be allowed to blind even a son-in-law. It's only kind to Ambrose — only fair to him, really — to protect him from the consequences of hanging on to an attitude that was common enough to his generation, but that sticks in the craw of our contemporaries. I'm talking, of course, of his virulent anti-Semitism, which is obviously the core of his objection to Morris Applebaum's firm. And that kind of thing, believe me, isn't going to do us a bit of good in a world where racial and religious intolerance has become the blackest of all crimes. Perhaps, indeed, the only one that people take really seriously anymore!"

Was this fair to Ambrose? Harry was a bit taken aback at how successful some of these little chats had been. He knew through an indignant Vinnie that her father had been much upset by that talk at the lunch club and that he had even gone so far as to consult one of his old Jewish friends to ask if his attitude was really as bad as Harry had tried to make out. After which he had discussed with one of his older partners the possibility of dropping any kind of hiring quotas. But wasn't the very fact that he still regarded it as a matter to be discussed evidence of the continuance of an attitude of extreme prejudice?

Of course it was! And he *was* being fair to Ambrose! Harry had to remind himself that those who feared the heat should stay clear of kitchens. Empire builders couldn't be overdelicate about the rights of aborigines. And at this point he was in the home stretch of the question of merger. If he wavered now, the whole issue would be lost. Morris Applebaum, impatient, was already hinting at merger talks with another corporate law firm.

The crisis broke on the afternoon of young Ambrose's baptism, which was to take place on the terrace of the Vollards' house in Glenville on a beautiful clear spring day where one could see all the way across Long Island Sound to the Connecticut shore. Before Vinnie and the minister had arrived with the boy and her daughters, Harry, who had made a point of being early, sought a private interview with his father-in-law in the library.

Ambrose listened in a surprised silence as his son-in-law for the first time explained his desire to change the boy's last name. Only when Harry spoke of Rod's lack of interest in the child did he interrupt.

"I have always intended, when the boy was a little older, to speak to Rod about that. Of course, I haven't seen Rod recently, but I'm told he's leading a perfectly respectable life, and he's certainly shown no neglect of either of his daughters. Rod may have changed, Harry. He may have come to regret what he has done to us. And if that is the case, he may wish in time to become acquainted with his son. We don't know what it was that made him turn from the child. I have a funny sort of idea that he may have associated the baby with his own sin. That he may be mortally ashamed of having been an adulterer when the child was conceived."

Harry was jarred. Could the old man really believe that? "But whether or not that is the case, sir, the fact remains that your grandson is left in my care and that I am the one charged with his rearing. It is really only just that he should bear my name."

"Even if it makes people talk? For they will, you know."

"I don't see why they should. Lots of children today take their stepfather's name."

"But not under these exact circumstances."

"Circumstances are never exactly the same."

Ambrose turned to face his son-in-law squarely at this. "Are you asking my permission?"

"No sir. The decision is mine and your daughter's."

"And Vinnie is for it?"

Harry hesitated. "She is not against it."

"Then I have no more to say."

Harry was about to protest, but Ambrose vouchsafed no further word and took his way out of the house by a French win-

117

dow to the terrace where Vinnie and the minister had just arrived, and the few friends invited had already gathered.

After the brief ceremony champagne was served. Little Ambrose, grasping with one hand the string of a large red balloon, grinned at the company while holding tight with his other to his stepfather's. Nobody had expressed the least surprise at the announced change of name. Indeed, it had probably been expected.

Ambrose stood apart from the group, glass in hand, looking deeply preoccupied. This also surprised nobody, for his recent moodiness was well known to the small community. But Harry noted uneasily how his glance wandered occasionally from his grandson's features to those of his son-in-law. Was he at long last noting something? Well, why not, for God's sake?

Nothing more happened until Harry and Vinnie were leaving with their family. Ambrose took his son-in-law suddenly by the cuff and pulled him away out of earshot of the others.

"All right, you can have your fucking merger!" he snarled, and, turning abruptly on his heel, went into the house.

If, on a visit to the cathedral at Chartres, the Virgin had leaned down from her window over the altar to spit that word at him, Harry could not have been more shocked.

10

❧

The five years that brought glory to Harry also brought fame and fortune to Rodman Jessup. He had hardly settled himself in a new apartment, and adjusted himself to the life of a divorced parent who took his daughters to the movies or the zoo on Saturday afternoons, when he was invited to lunch by an old law school classmate, Newbold Armstrong, in a newly formed club atop a skyscraper in midtown, whither much of the Wall and Broad Street legal and financial community were already beginning to move. Armstrong, the handsome, clean-cut scion of an old New York clan, was a partner in a new and aggressive law firm that was making a rather notorious name for itself in the burgeoning field of the proxy fights attending the formation of corporate conglomerates. After one cocktail and a brief and perfunctory inquiry into his old friend's health and family, Armstrong came right to the point. Would Rod consider a partnership in his firm?

Rod restrained the initial impulse to wrinkle his nose. "I'm not a great fan of proxy fights. Some of them strike me as verging on dirty pool. I'm sorry to say that, Newbold, but you and I may as well be frank with each other. At Vollard Kaye we used to turn down those retainers."

"Vollard Kaye is beginning to show its age, my friend. And

you'll soon enough see the truth of that. Survival these days consists in keeping up with the times. Luckily for me the Armstrongs always made a point of that. One of my grandfathers acted as broker for 'Uncle' Dan Drew, the greatest rascal on Wall Street. And a great-aunt of mine married a son of Jay Gould, whom no respectable family would let into their house by the front door. And look at us now! We're doing just fine, thank you. I had rather hoped, Rod, that the way you'd been treated by your old firm and family-in-law, for doing what three quarters of the men I know have done at one point or another in their lives, would have opened your eyes. Of course, I have to admit that you weren't very tactful in the way you went about it. But that was probably because you'd always been such a Christer. You hadn't learned that it's not what you do that counts. It's how you do it."

Rod fixed a long silent stare on his luncheon host. "You know, Newbold, there may be something in what you say."

"There's a hell of a lot in what I say."

"Won't it create bitterness among the associates in your firm if you take in a partner from outside ahead of them?"

"Oh, I daresay they won't like it. But they're used to it. Everyone 'buys' partners from the outside these days. The only man who'll really mind is the partner we'll be dumping if we get hold of you."

"Why him? What's he done?"

"It's what he's not done. His billings don't add up, Rod. The days are gone when a firm will keep on some old geezer who's ceased to produce. We're not a retirement home, after all. I'll bet that Vollard Kaye has some old farts on its payroll who've been eating free off it for years."

Rod nodded grimly. "Probably. And of course the same thing would happen to me in your firm if I didn't pan out."

"And to me, too!" Newbold cheerfully agreed. "But I'm betting on us. Who wants special treatment? Come to us, Rod, and I'll count on you to become our star man in a proxy holocaust."

"What makes you think I'd be so good at it?"

His friend still chose to make a joke of it. His laugh was loud and free. "Because I can see that after the way you've been treated you're just about ready to take off the mask. You're not Little Red Riding Hood's granny anymore, buddy. You're the big bad wolf himself!"

Rod took the job, and in two years' time he had gained the reputation of being one of the toughest proxy battlers in the city.

On saturdays, when Rod called at the Hammerslys' commodious Park Avenue apartment to pick up his daughters, Harry and Vinnie had the tact always to be out, or at least invisible in their private quarters. But one day, when he was ushered into the living room, he found Vinnie sitting there alone, rather tensely smiling and considerably stouter than when he had last seen her. She rose and stepped forward to greet him with an extended hand.

"The girls will be down in a minute," she assured him. "But I wanted a word with you first. I hope you don't mind."

"Why should I mind?"

"Good. Shall we sit? It's just this. Harry wants to talk to you on a business matter. But he wasn't sure you'd be willing to see him. So he asked me to feel out the ground."

Rod frowned. Could it be about money? Was anything wrong between her and Harry? "Tell me about your life. Things are going well in your marriage?"

"I guess you're entitled to ask that." Her short affirmative nod expressed a willingness to return to the candor of their earlier relationship. "Well enough, anyway. The bloom is off the rose, but that was to be expected. We live like two civilized beings. Harry, as I'm sure you always knew, is a bit of a shit, but there are two kinds of that breed: the ones who are perfectly agreeable when they get what they want and the ones who continue to be disagreeable even then. Harry is the first kind. He's an easy man to live with. I only hope it stays that way."

"I suppose there's no reason it shouldn't. What does he want of me?"

"I don't know, but you can be sure it will be something to your advantage. Whatever Harry is, he's no fool."

"Tell him to call me. Any time."

Harry's manner, when he met Rod for lunch, was as easy as ever. He didn't manifest any of the embarrassment that even such a sophisticate as he must have felt. Rod was gratified to note that even when he recalled the acts that Harry and Vinnie had performed together, as recorded in her infamous journal, he experienced no anger and little disgust. He had moved decisively into a different world.

Harry did not beat around the bush any more than Newbold Armstrong had two years earlier. He wanted Rod to come back to Vollard Kaye at double the pay he was receiving from the Armstrong firm. As to his position in the partnership he could pretty well write his own ticket. Harry made it clear that they needed him badly, not only to set up an acquisitions branch in the corporate department but to assist Harry in further modernizing the administration of the firm. Rod was impressed by Harry's cleverness in realizing that a blunt statement of the difficulties of the firm was the best way to handle the man who had once been expelled from it. Harry was smart enough to see that Rod wanted more than anything else to triumph over the world that Rod himself had maneuvered into excluding him.

"But how about Ambrose?" Rod wanted to know. "How will he feel about taking back an ex-son-in-law?"

"Ambrose will not be a problem. Ambrose is not the man he was. You probably know about the stroke he had a month ago, and though he's recovered his speech and pretty much the use of his arms and legs, he's a shadow of his old self. I've discussed you with him, and he's taken it all like a lamb, just nodding his head."

"He still comes to the office?"

"Yes, but only from habit and to look at his mail. He does no work of any significance. Glances over his trustees' accountings. That sort of thing. I even showed him that nasty cartoon of you in that rag *The Unconfidential Clerk*, and he only smiled."

"Why did you show him that?" The periodical in question, hated by the big law firms, purported to show the clerks exactly how their employers operated. The cartoon had depicted Rod on his knees by an overturned garbage pail, ransacking its contents for dirt on some company a client of his was seeking to harass into submission.

"Because if that rag has it in for you, it means you're the hottest thing in proxy fights!"

As little as a year later Rod was installed in the largest office of the firm, now renamed Vollard, Hammersly & Jessup, at the end of a corridor containing the adjoining offices of the two partners and four associates, all corporate experts, whom he had induced to sever their ties with Armstrong and join him in his new affiliation. His old friend and former partner, Newbold, had wildly threatened to sue him, but everyone knew it was an idle threat, and Rod had thrown back at him his own words about keeping up with the times.

Ambrose, poor broken old man, had greeted him joyously, as if no cloud had ever darkened their covering sky. Though confined to a wheelchair, he loved to come to the office and lunch with any of the partners whom Harry Hammersly could induce to spare the time. He took to wheeling himself into Rod's office to chat about the past, and the latter's time so wasted became a bit of a problem, but Rod was still determined that this was not one of the times that had to be kept up with. His love of his former father-in-law was a surviving remnant of his old faith.

Harry showed no sign of jealousy at Rod's immediate success in the firm: had it not been his own idea? Even Rod was now becoming convinced that Harry would even accept his surpassing him as managing partner, provided that the net profits of all were substantially increased. Rod had learned in the Armstrong firm to bow to the principle that the question of compensation took precedence over everything else, and he no longer even wanted to interfere with Harry's rigid rule requiring every lawyer in the firm to live up to the number of profitable hours per week assigned to him, nor did he complain when Harry hired partners and clerks from the outside and placed them ahead of workers already in the vineyard. Was Rod himself not the prime example of the practice?

He and Harry lunched together regularly twice a week, and he found himself once again succumbing to Harry's charm. He even agreed, at Harry's urging, to take a case out of his usual field.

"Face it, Rod," Harry had insisted, over his second martini at their lunch club, "the firm is now fairly well under your and my control. And we're certainly equipped to handle it, except, if you will allow one small suggestion, that you need a bit more experience in the area of individual clients. I'd like you to try your hand at a different sort of case. In our trust and estates department. A big society divorce."

"Oh, Harry, no. You know how I hate that. Two cats using, or abusing, the law to scratch each other's eyes out."

"And that's so different from what you do?"

"Completely. What I wage is war. Not vendetta."

"Well, I don't make your fine distinctions. To me law is law. And this case will help to make your name known in the social circles that still haven't lost all their glitter in this changing town. I suppose even a hick like you has heard of the Farquars."

The family was a remnant of Mrs. Astor's famed Four Hundred, which had not lost its grip on acres of precious Manhattan soil. "Of course. Paul is the present heir, is he not?"

"He is. And old Paul wants his freedom to marry some little tramp. And his beautiful and charming consort, the toast of the crème de la crème, has been persuaded by yours truly that she needs more aggressive counsel."

"Really, Harry. Aren't you afraid of the ethics committee?"

"Don't worry, my pal. I do those things with a subtlety that would stand up before the saintliest martinet. I guarantee that you will find Jane Farquar a fascinating client. And I think she will appreciate a lawyer who's not only as sharp as she is, but a good-looking fellow to boot."

"Must I make love to her? Isn't there something in the canons about that?"

"There's nothing in the canons about marrying her."

"Oh, Harry! Is there no length to which we must not go to hang on to a client?" But he decided to let it pass as a joke. "All right, brief me. What are the rights and wrongs in Farquar versus Farquar?"

Harry briefed him. And the very next day the two of them called on Jane Farquar at her splendid Fifth Avenue duplex. Rod had tried to persuade Harry that it was undignified for them not to request her to come to their office, but Harry had insisted that it was a question of the exception proving the rule.

The long noble rectangular chamber overlooking Central Park in which they awaited Mrs. Farquar was an ample introduction to the eclectic good taste of their new client. The dark paneling and carved white ceiling were Jacobean, the giant teakwood commode and chairs were Chinese, the carpet a magnificent Turk and on one wall a Turner seascape harmonized with a Gauguin of a Tahiti beach. It was more the collection of a woman with a perfectly trained eye than an art lover. One felt it might all be changed the next season.

Rod's first impression when the lady came briskly in, flashing on them a friendly yet formal smile, was, appropriately enough, a golden one. Her neatly brushed hair, whose color could have been natural, as she was still just under forty, was a fine golden blond, and she relieved the raven blackness of her dress with heavy gold jewelry: a bracelet, a necklace and globular earrings. Her features were almost too regular for her reputed beauty, but her eyes argued a mitigation of the severity of her perfection: they were an enchanting sky blue and seemed to make a case for her essential humanity. Her manner was cordial, but it was still evident that the two men to whom such cordiality was offered were on probation. Her lawyer, of course, was expected to be among the first in his profession.

The three now discussed the best approach to the problem of a settlement. Rod had learned the salient fact that Mrs. Farquar had signed a prenuptial agreement, approved by her then eminent counsel, in which she had agreed to accept three million dollars in the event of a divorce, regardless of the alleged fault of either party. There was always the danger, he had now to point out, that if the matter went to court, a judge or jury might limit her to that amount.

"Which means, of course, Mr. Jessup," Jane countered coolly, "that we must prevail out of court. I have no objection to freeing my husband to marry the little slut who's got hold of him, but I fully expect to be left just as well off without him as I was with him. And three million isn't going to begin to do the trick. In addition to what he has already settled on me, I shall need at least another ten."

Rod noted that they were not even to discuss the question of her being morally bound to honor a contract into which she had freely entered. Litigation was to be the same with individuals as it was with corporations.

"Then the only thing we have to fear is his establishing a valid residence in an easy divorce state and obtaining a decree there without your appearance or consent. Then, if you sued him in New York, you might be held to the damages stipulated in the prenuptial agreement, although of course we'd claim fraud and misrepresentation of assets and everything else under the sun. But he would have to really live in that state — no phony Reno six-week stay. Is there any danger that he might really quit New York?"

"I doubt it. The family estate up the Hudson is sacred to him. And he's always had a crazy idea that he might run for the state senate from up there."

"Then I think we can really make him pay. I take it he has no grounds for divorce in New York?"

"None whatever. My record is white as snow."

"Then he's blocked. And if he remarries after an out-of-state divorce we'll have him for bigamy. I take it you'll give me a free hand in the matter?"

"Throw the book at him, Mr. Jessup. And the harder you hit, the better. And now, gentlemen, can I offer you a drink?"

Rod, in his accustomed fashion, gave the job his all. Detectives were hired to uncover every bit of dirt in Paul Farquar's rather shabby past. The smell of such items was even more important than their truth; as missiles they could be used to humiliate his family as well as himself, and, in particular, the children of his first two marriages. Happily, none had been born to Jane. The inventory of Paul's wealth submitted to Jane's counsel before their marriage, however detailed, was subject to minute scrutiny and attack, and Rod even put aside, as a desperate last remedy, an indication that Paul had once suffered from a venereal disease. Could he threaten that it had been communicated to his client? he asked her.

"Only if all else fails," she replied with a laugh.

Rod was enjoying himself. He relished his interviews with this always amusing and charming woman. It had become an item of the first importance to him to win her case for her, not only for the glory of his practice, but to prove that he was just as sharp and ruthless a fighter as she obviously expected a man — *her* type of man, anyway — to be.

The intimate nature of their discussions — such, for example, as the imputed gonorrhea, though each knew it had *not* been transmitted — inevitably led to a closer, a more congenial, relationship, and Rod soon found himself invited to one of Jane's large dinner parties and happily accepting. Her friends, many of whose names were familiar to readers of society news, were an amalgam of the world of arts, decoration, haute couture and moneymaking. The gentleman Rod found himself talking to at cocktails might turn out to be a playwright, psychiatrist or investment banker; the lady a perfume queen, actress or fashion magazine editor. All were successful, smartly clad, well mannered and thoroughly at ease with each other.

And Rod noticed something else about them, as he came to be more and more included in Jane's lively social life. They did not indulge in the habit of detrimental anecdote so often attributed to social circles. On the contrary, admission to Jane's brilliant group seemed to require a constant round of mutual admiration. "Isn't Mike wonderful?" or "Have you ever seen Helenka in better form?" was the kind of remark he heard as he passed through the room. This, he noted, was even truer when the individual commented upon had little to his credit but a larger fortune or famous name, in which case the company endowed him with a virtue, not immediately apparent to a neutral eye, which was the "real" cause of his inclusion. Only a rude observer would have speculated on the rapacity that might have marked the earlier years of some of them or suggested that the state of their souls might be less elegant than their manners or looks.

Jane took to asking him to stay on for a nightcap after her other guests had left, and nobody, of course, appeared to take the least notice of this. She also invited him on occasion to accompany her to dinners given by her friends. Her husband, under Rod's relentless pressure, was beginning to show signs of weakening resistance to his wife's exorbitant demands, and Rod and Jane were now more relaxed in conversations which no longer had to focus on her case.

Less intent now on demonstrating to her his skill as a lawyer, Rod could concentrate more on impressing her as a man. If her wealth and social position had promoted a rather vulgar desire in him to show her that he was her equal, her charm and beauty had turned this into the equally crude wish to be her master. But now something much more benign seemed to be happening to him. It was simply that he was falling in love.

For too long a time now he had lived in a kind of proud and resentful chastity. It was as if he had come to deem himself superior to the demands and preoccupations of sex. But it was certainly intensely agreeable to feel that this immensely sympathetic and widely popular woman was frankly interested in him.

He quite understood that what most intrigued her about himself was the aura of masculine ruthlessness that she imagined him to emit. By instinct as well as by will, he had taken to making the most of this.

"Practicing law, as I do it, seems to satisfy something basic in my nature," he told her on one of their late nights. "It's a kind of zest for combat that some unlucky men seem unable to get out of their systems."

"And women."

"Do you feel it too? It doesn't really surprise me. You strike me as having a touch of Semiramis or Boadicea in you."

"Is that a compliment?"

"From me it is. I don't mind that in a woman. And I wonder if a certain native combativeness in a man isn't more attractive than its total absence."

"Oh, I agree with you! I can't stand wishy washies. We seem to be forgetting these days that a man's not a real man unless there's a bit of a brute in him. And you needn't look at me that way. I'm perfectly aware that I'm politically incorrect. I share all the old Wasp values, and I glory in it!"

Rod thought she was going a bit far, even for him, but he didn't dislike it. He wondered if she wouldn't make love like a lioness, snarling at and scratching her mate. He became graver. "Brooks Adams maintained in his *Law of Civilization and Decay* that the warrior class is bound eventually to be replaced by the usurer. The crusaders were noble but futile; they had to fall before the moneylender. We must bow to history, I suppose, and accept the world as it is. But I like to think I can find in the battle of the corporate takeover some faint remnant of the warrior spirit. It's a way of playing the old game of kill or be killed without breaking any law. Harmless, isn't it? Or is it?"

"I like that!" she exclaimed with enthusiasm. "And I don't give a damn if it's not harmless!"

The way she looked at him now made him wonder if Harry had not been right in the first place. Was Harry going to take over his life again?

"I haven't told you, Jane," he now informed her, "because it's still not definite. But I think we can expect your husband's total surrender in a matter of days."

She leaned forward to kiss him on the cheek. "My hero! My Vercingetorix." And then she broke into a hearty laugh. "But will there be anything left of my settlement when I've paid your fee?"

He smiled. "There'll be me."

11

❧

WHAT JANE HAD BEGUN to realize, in the year following her debutante party in 1937, was that if she didn't somehow break away from the appalling normalcy of her family, she would be condemned to become appallingly normal herself. She was under no misapprehension that her parents were as expertly adapted to cope with their environment as polar bears to the Arctic or camels to the desert. The Seatons lived in a standard Manhattan brownstone, furnished tastefully but unsurprisingly by W. & J. Sloane, and a small shingle villa on the dunes in the Hamptons. Daddy, a stockbroker who had made some money in the roaring twenties but had put just enough into treasuries to survive the Depression, even in a much depleted fashion, was a kind if undemonstrative parent, moderately content with the golfing weekends he could just still afford, with his easy if poorly remunerated office routine and his long downtown martini-laced lunches. Mummy, whose smiles and sympathy almost made up for her voids in humor and imagination, divided her time innocuously between her family and the bridge table. Jane had "leaked out" at a modest tea dance at home and was now taking courses in art appreciation while waiting for "Mr. Right" to come along. The usual noisy and impudent kid brother was at Groton.

But that was not all. It did not take in the ease with which they compromised with the less lovable aspects of their era and class. Jane's parents were, of course, good Republicans, but they never went overboard in hating FDR; they even dared to hint that he might have forestalled a social revolution. As Christians they were Episcopalians and went to church on rainy Sundays, but they had no theological tenets and gave little more than lip service to the conventional anti-Semitic and anti-Catholic prejudices of their friends. The motto they might have chosen, "Nothing in excess," extended to their enthusiasms as well as their dislikes: art and literature were welcomed but not embraced; self-sacrificing devotion to worthy causes was admired but not emulated. On the whole, they liked the world, and the world, on the whole, liked them.

Where Jane made out at last that she would have to break with their values was in their attitude towards the "great world" of society, on the fringes of which they precariously lived. Nothing in the world would have persuaded Sophia or Gridley Seaton that they were in the least snobbish or even worldly, qualities that they roundly deplored. Why then, their daughter wanted to know, did they belong to the most restricted clubs and send their children to the most restricted schools; why was their acquaintance limited to the Social Register and their summers to the swankiest beach resort? Why? they repeated. Why, because they always *had*. It had nothing to do with what they thought or whom they respected. And what really upset them in Jane's attitude was not, as with so many privileged children of the Depression, that she had gone so far left — that was so common as to be almost respectable — but that she had gone so far right!

Jane had observed, with a realistic eye and a bitter heart, just how the Depression had cut into her family's life style, just what sacrifices had had to be made to keep up the appearance of gentility. She had known what it was to be on a scholarship in a rich girls' school, to have few dresses amid the dressy, to have to give up the beach club and rely on the invitations of the supercilious. She saw that in a world of multifold discomforts the well-to-do were the only ones unaffected, and she made it her resolve that one day she would be numbered among them. It was not that she did not perfectly see what hash so many of the wealthy made of their lives, but they were fools, and whatever Jane was destined to become, it was not that. Marriage was the only viable out, and fortunately her family's proximity to the palaces of prosperity offered ample opportunity.

Families note everything. As Oliver Wendell Holmes observed, you can't fool a regular boarder. Sophia Seaton was well aware of her daughter's cultivation of the richer among her old classmates and at last reproached her for it. But she was hardly prepared for Jane's stinging retort.

"Haven't you brought me up cheek by jowl with people who had all the things we didn't? How could I be expected not to try to be a part of them?"

"I expected that you might try to use your good brain and the advantages of an excellent education to make a decent place for yourself in the world," was her mother's tart reply. Sophia, behind a placid front, had preserved some old values. "It had not occurred to me that the spectacle of a few show-offs marking a display of their new money would go to your head. You've always had the things that mattered: a good home, good teachers, good friends and all the comforts a girl could need. Don't be always looking up, my dear. Look down and see the millions who haven't a fraction of what you've had!"

"What can you gain by looking down? You might even drop! But looking up, you might find a ladder somewhere."

"A ladder! Don't tell me that a child of mine could ever

become a social climber!" Sophia's pride was now aroused. After all, the Seatons weren't nothing. "I wonder, child, if you haven't inherited some of the genes of my Grandmother Bane. We used to marvel at the crudity of some of her social assessments. It wasn't as if she had been born on the wrong side of the tracks. She had been a Babcock, which, as the French say, was *assez bien*. But I remember that when I told her I didn't like a particular friend of hers, an old lady called Mrs. Dows, who for some reason had been mean to me, she retorted, 'You mustn't say that. Mrs. Dows has three million dollars.'"

"But that must have been a huge fortune in those days!" Jane exclaimed. "Great-Grandma Bane had simply the candor to express what the rest of you were all thinking! Yes, I think I *have* some of her genes. And I'm proud of it!"

"Jane, Jane, what are we going to do with you?" her mother wailed.

Jane lived in a world where there were plenty of rich young men, but they were inclined to be edgy about girls with the reputation of looking for what they had, and Jane had found herself furnished with such a taint, no doubt by some girls with the same objective. She was eventually to find what she needed, but not before she had made one seemingly fatal mistake.

Tommy Seitz had no money, but everyone seemed to assume that he would make a fortune. He certainly had no doubts about it himself. He had everything in the world that was desirable except money. He was handsome, athletic, bright, witty, cheerful and good tempered, a popular member of his Yale class, elected to the distinguished secret society of Scroll & Key, a champion squash player and now the promising employee of a known investment banking firm. And he shunned all the heiresses at the Southampton Beach Club to devote himself to the beautiful but penniless Jane, who had only appeared there as a guest! It would have broken a harder resolution than hers, and it now broke her determination to limit herself to the ugly and awkward son of a shipping magnate who, despite his mother's disapproval, had been showing her timid attention. For Tommy, it appeared, was really serious and not the idle philanderer she had first taken him to be.

Yes, he had actually proposed! Could she still care that his family were a good deal dimmer and simpler than her own? She could only assume that some bright-colored cuckoo bird had deposited an alien egg in their dingy nest.

He was bravely candid about himself.

"All my friends have taken for granted that I would make what is called a great match. But what's the use of a fortune if one hasn't a beautiful and enchanting spouse to spend it with? You and I are a pair marked for the role. Don't you see it? Will you be willing to take your chances with me?"

Jane thought she did see it. She also assumed that she was in love, as it was hard for her not to imagine herself in love with such a swain as Tom. And this despite her uneasy and constantly stifled small suspicion that there was something wrong with him, that he was another Tom Seitz pretending to be the Tom Seitz she was seeing before her. But if he didn't know it himself . . . !

Shortly after they were married he was off to the wars as executive officer of a sub chaser, and this added to his romantic glow. But when peace returned, it seemed to have brought a turn in his luck. Not only was she faced with the unexpected barrenness of her marriage — though there seemed no physical reason for it — she was confronted with the barrenness of their means. Tom changed from company to company with a consistent lack of success, while spending freely on the hectic and supposedly brilliant social life that he insisted was essential to his business ventures.

After two years of such a life he announced to her blandly that he was dead broke. He did not seem surprised or even depressed by the fact. He proceeded to outline what he called "Plan B" as coolly as if she, a presumably cool partner, would at once recognize its inevitability.

"It hasn't worked, my love. It simply hasn't worked."

"What hasn't worked?"

"Our marriage. My whole initial scheme. I've had a vicious stream of bad luck, which no one could have visualized, and now I have no credit to seek further capital with. There's only one way I can get it, and that is by a rich marriage."

Jane felt something more like awe than outrage. She stared at the monster before her and realized that she had never known him to be anything but the appearance of what he was not.

"Are you telling me that you want a divorce?" she asked, almost in curiosity.

"Not that I want it, but I have no choice. Any more than you do. We both have to seek new and rich spouses while we still have a modicum of youth and beauty."

She saw now that she must have long suspected that she was wed to a man, like the Tin Woodman of the Oz books, who had no heart. But unlike the Tin Woodman Tom had no concept of his lack; he did not know what a heart was, yet some basic instinct had taught him to conceal this fact from a world in which it might not have found favor. She found herself marveling that he could have kept up so brave a show before all his friends — if indeed any of his acquaintance could really be called that. Could a monster have friends? Could a monster be loved? Even by his wife? Oh, certainly not by his wife! And yet . . . could a monster really help being what he was?

"And who have you selected for a better mate?" she asked.

"Oh, I think Ella Ripley will have me. In fact, I think I may say I'm sure of it."

"So? You've been at work already. And who, may I ask, have you picked for me? Or am I left to do my own work? You might have given me more warning. It's much easier to attract a man behind a marriage than after a divorce."

"But are you blind, my dear? Everyone knows Paul Farquar is gaga about you! He may be a trifle long in the tooth, and he's got two failed marriages behind him, but he'll give you a position second to none in the whole damn town! And what you say about operating better as a married woman than a divorcée is absolutely true. Ella can wait — so long as I keep her satisfied — and you can have all the time you need to hook Paul. I'm sure I don't have to warn you not to let the old goat have his way with you until the ring is firmly on your finger."

Paul Farquar was a gruff, dour man of fifty with short curly gray hair and a bulldog countenance, who had never tried to please and rarely succeeded. His abruptness of manner and rudeness of speech would not have been tolerated in a man of less wealth, but the Farquars, thanks in part to the indefatigable party-giving and high pretensions of his late mother and grandmother, enjoyed a unique social prestige in the city and, more importantly, in the press. Nor was Paul himself quite a nobody. He was intelligent, though his brain was largely unexercised, and he relished a proud nature that scorned anyone who made up to him. Jane had found his heavy streak of crude honesty not wholly unattractive.

Besides that, he was smitten by her. Assuming that he had only one thing in mind, she had shrugged off his brash compliments and insinuations, which had only the result of intensifying his interest, and now she decided to be more receptive. In far less time than the unspeakable Tom was willing to accord her she had her cantankerous admirer totally enslaved, and when the time came for the divorce the Farquar lawyers speeded the process to its happily predicted conclusion.

Of her dozen years as Mrs. Farquar Jane found adequate content in the first ten. She was able to perform her sexual role to her greedy spouse's satisfaction, however little to her own, and she learned how to stake out her own independent demesne in what had been his rigidly ordered and isolated life. For he was quite capable of being fair. In return for his paying for, and even his occasional presence at, her grand successful dinner parties, she agreed to their long, lonely visits to his castle on the Hudson or his shooting lodge in South Carolina. And in return for the seats on the opera and museum boards that he had "bought" for her, she winked at the occasional girlfriend who took her willingly abandoned place in his bed. An unimpeachable wife herself, steadied by what she gratefully conceived to be the coldness of her nature, she would have willingly played the role of Madame de Pompadour to Louis XV and established for him a discreet deer park, but he, ultimately sensing that he repelled her physically, preferred to find his own does. And, inevitably, in the end one of these turned out to be a more designing type who resolved to become Mrs. Farquar.

"Of course, I married Paul for his money," she had told her mother, when she informed the latter of the proposed divorce. "No woman in her right mind would have wed him for any other reason. But I was no ordinary gold digger. With me it was a contract. He gave me all the things I wanted, and I in return gave him the nearest thing to happiness he's ever had. He'll find that out when he marries his concubine. And I would have stuck to him, too, if he had allowed me to. But, as it is, I'm delighted to be free and on my own, and I certainly intend to make sure that he pays me damages in full for breaking our agreement. Isn't that only fair?"

"Don't ask me, my dear. I haven't a head for these things. You've always had your own way. I can only pray it's for the best."

U p   i n   a   b o x overlooking the dance floor of the Plaza's grand ballroom, Jane and Harry Hammersly, both members of the board of the charity hosting the benefit party, were showing little interest in the spectacle of the whirling couples. Only one of them held their attention. Rod Jessup was dancing with his ex-wife, Vinnie, and his expression made it clear that it was a duty dance.

"You'd better go down and cut in, Harry."

"Those whom God hath joined, let no man put asunder. Besides, I want to talk about Rod. Or rather about him and you."

"I'll tell you frankly that I like your partner, Harry." Jane spoke in her definite tone, which was very definite. "Of course, I perfectly saw that you wanted me to."

"How did you see that?"

"Because you never do anything without a purpose. Don't be offended. I have no objection to purposeful men. But I don't quite make out your motive. Is it to hang on to me as a client? Do you really think that, even if I were married to your handsome partner, I'd hesitate to leave your roster if I thought I wasn't getting the best legal advice available?"

"No, I know you too well. And don't *you* be offended. I have no objection to purposeful women. You could do much worse for a third husband than Rod."

"What do you know about my husbands? Oh, of course, you know about Paul. But did you ever meet Tom Seitz?"

"No. But I know he left you to marry an heiress."

"Just so. He was the one great mistake of my life. And I'm determined not to make another. My marriage to Paul may have broken up, but it was hardly a mistake."

"Hardly. With the princely settlement he's made you."

Jane did not quite like this. "I got much more than my settlement through Paul. But I don't expect you to see that." She looked at Harry now more closely. She and he shared something like a meeting of the minds. She considered herself a nicer person than he but not much nicer. "Do you want to make up to Rod for taking his wife? To buy your atonement with my money? No, that wouldn't really be like you, would it? You don't believe in atonement."

"Hardly," he said again. "I'm not trying to conceal anything from you, Jane. I worry about Rod. His temperament is so uncertain. I think it would help him — and help my firm, of course — if he were to find peace of mind, and settle down with a fine woman like you."

"Why, Harry! I'd no idea you could be so sentimental!"

"Sometimes it's realistic to be sentimental."

Jane was enjoying the subject. She was enjoying it intensely. She didn't care if Harry repeated everything she said, as he well might. "And now tell me what's in it for a fine woman like me."

"A first-class husband. A noble soul."

"Well!" She threw back her head as she laughed. "That from you, my friend, must be a real compliment. But why did this noble soul cheat on his wife?"

"I can only suppose that he suspected that she was cheating on him."

"And was she?"

He hesitated. "Yes."

"I wonder with whom." Again she laughed. "At least, Harry, you know that a mortifying truth is better to make your point with than a detectable lie. So I'll be equally frank with you. I do really like your partner. I may even be a bit in love with him. I find him Byronic. Like a corsair." Here she quoted from memory.

> "He knew himself detested, but he knew
> The hearts that loathed him crouched and dreaded, too.
> Lone, wild and strange he stood alike exempt
> From all affection and from all contempt."

B<small>UT HE HAD A HEART</small>, didn't he?" Harry demanded.

"Oh, certainly. A Byronic hero has to have *that*."

"If I'm sentimental, Jane, is it so odd that you should be romantic?"

"But I'm a realistic romantic, Harry. I'm not a dream-crazed female who sees Lancelot in every handsome profile that pays her the least attention. I've reached an age of wisdom and achieved a fortune with which to implement it. I think I know just how to play all the cards in my hand — and in my heart, too — to find the kind of real happiness I want. I shan't be fooled again."

"Rap on wood when you say that."

"Why, Harry, don't you approve?"

"One always has second thoughts when a dearly held project is about to succeed."

"How like you, my friend! You can never really believe in anything, even something you've done your damnedest to bring about!"

"Call it my curse. Believe it or not, my dear, I'm actually thinking of you. Rod can be quite something to handle."

"Leave him to me. I know what he is."

"Are you so sure?"

12

JANE FARQUAR, NOW JANE JESSUP, had hitherto assumed
that she was adequately equipped to handle any crisis that was
apt to occur in her adequately protected life. This had certainly
been true in her first two marriages. But her third had presented questions for which she seemed to have no easily available response. The bewildering aspect of her situation was that
she seemed to have fallen in love — and that for the first time
in her life. She had been pretty well convinced that such was a
state of mind — or of heart or whatever it was — that would
never happen to her, except insofar as her girlish flutters over
Tom Seitz could have been called that. Nor had she in the least
objected to such apparent immunity to the arrows of Eros. She
had always regarded herself as a priestess of the life of reason
and was quite content to remain that.

But now she was faintly disgusted to find herself fussing and
fretting over the novel business not of being a dutiful wife —
she had been that — but of being a loving wife. And it was certainly not that Rod had brought her any of the obvious trou-
bles that a new mate might bring. He had moved without the
slightest protest into her duplex apartment, and had been willing to go out to her Long Island villa on the few weekends
when he wasn't tied to his office. He had indeed accepted with-

out a murmur her whole regimen of life: the servants, the cars, even the dinner parties (when he wasn't working late). He didn't change the position of a single chair or table or even suggest the rehanging of a picture. She had first supposed that his own possession of a large earned income freed him from any petty jealousy of his wife's greater wealth, but she soon made out that it was rather a complete indifference on his part to money and things. He neither desired nor sought them; they simply didn't exist for him. It was true that he was very careful to receive a lion's share of his firm's income, but this was more to retain his reputation among the law firms than anything else.

As a domestic partner, in contrast to a legal one, he was above reproach. He treated her with a grave and kindly courtesy that she found utterly charming, listened with apparently sincere sympathy to all her enthusiasms and complaints, and rarely showed the least sign of irritation or temper. He was always firmly supportive. Yet he never flirted with her, never gave her the eye, and rarely even touched her except to guide her elbow walking on the street or assist her in donning or doffing a cloak. This might have worried or even alarmed her, had he not in bed made silent and fiercely passionate love to her. He never, however, on the morrow made any reference to these couplings. Did he forget them? Was he even perhaps a bit ashamed of them? She didn't know, and somehow didn't dare to ask. She felt like Psyche, visited only in the dark.

Did he really love her? But if he didn't, why had he married her? Or was it just for those nights? Was he capable of love? Certainly, if his obsession with his office work could be called love, he was. She had learned early that he would grant her any request except one that would interfere with his professional routine, but this routine was so pressing that the field of his favors to her was considerably limited. To have asked him to give up a single night's work for a dinner party would have been like asking a surgeon to desert his operating table, and she had known better than to try.

But at least in their first year Jane, on the whole, was contented with her lot. She had learned to amuse and interest herself with her board memberships in the long and unregretted absences of her second husband, so she never found time on her hands, no matter how tied up Rod was with his litigation. But in time she began to suffer from the greed that is always in store for those who are doomed to wreck their own good fortune, and she started to give in to the temptations of petulance over the fact that she didn't share a greater part of her husband's life.

She had never been one to put much trust in the discretion of woman friends — particularly in the smart set in which she moved — and through the years, oddly enough, she had come to rely as the recipient of her confidences on a mother with whom, as a girl, she had not been very congenial. But a mother, after all, is always a mother.

"I know it's the fate of many American wives to become what are called business widows," she told her parent one noon when Sophia had come to lunch. "But of course I never had to face that with Tom, who found only disaster in business, or Paul, who didn't have any. But Rod is married to that law firm of his."

"Then he's surely a bigamist, for he's certainly married to you, my dear, and happily married, too. Don't rock the boat!" Sophia didn't like to show too much how deeply she savored her enjoyment of these lunches *à deux* in the cool Pompeian dining nook with its elegant service. She had come little enough to her daughter's in the days of Tom, whom she had disliked, or of Paul, who had disliked her — as he had disliked everything pertaining to a bride whom he had wished to receive, so to speak, stripped of all remnants of a non-Farquar past. Rod had struck Sophia as the very welcome but quite undeserved final achievement of her daughter's distressingly worldly life. But all was well that ended well. Or was it?

Jane ignored the maternal warning. "Did you never find Daddy too taken up with his downtown life?"

"Well, I don't suppose many brokers of his day were quite as passionate about their trade as some lawyers are. Your father wouldn't have worked a minute after five P.M. if our whole future had depended on it. If I was jealous of anything it was his weekend golf. But it's not wise, my dear, to get between a man and his toys. It's like finding yourself between a hippo and the water. There are a lot of worse things that a man can get into besides his job."

But Jane was not going to be shuffled off by any reference to banal triangles. "Oh, if you mean another woman, I think I'd know how to handle that. It's not playing a secondary role in Rod's life that really worries me. It's wondering if I'm really playing any role at all."

"Oh, Jane dear, how can you even suggest such a thing?" Sophia was at last reluctantly alerted to the fact that there *was* a problem. "Rod's crazy about you! Anyone can see that."

"Anyone but me," Jane muttered, half to herself. "Maybe he's just crazy."

"You know what you should do? You should have a baby. That would settle all these silly morbid doubts. Then you'd have something better to worry about than how much your husband loves you."

"Mother, something that didn't happen with two difficult but far from impotent husbands isn't apt to happen with a third. Nor do I think it would particularly help. Rod has two perfectly good children, and I've never craved motherhood. No, my problem is different." As she went on, she was no longer hoping for any illumination from her friendly, worried and uninteresting parent, but she felt the need of an ear, and did she have any other? "What I think may be really wrong is that I'm going through the gushings and palpitations that I should have gone through at fifteen. And that I actually despise the silly little girl, so long repressed, who's trying to take me over. I was so determined that I was not going to be like you or Daddy or brother Bobby that I didn't see what I was doing to myself."

"Poor Bobby," her mother murmured. "You have certainly not been like him."

Bobby Seaton, for all his boyish charm, had not made a success of his career as a broker in the paternal firm or of either of his two broken marriages, and now lived largely on Jane's generous handouts. She was fully, if perhaps a bit complacently aware that her mother's gratitude for these had gone a long way to silence any articulated disapprovals of what she considered her daughter's too worldly espousals.

"Do you know what Rod's been doing for Bobby lately?" Sophia demanded suddenly, as if a ray of light had suddenly pierced the window blind of doubts that her perverse daughter insisted on lowering over her third and at last commendable marriage.

"No. What?"

"I thought you didn't. It's so like Rod to hide his light under a bushel. He's taken Bobby twice out to lunch to discuss his future with him. He doesn't feel that Bobby was really cut out to be a stockbroker. When Bobby told him he'd always had a hankering to do something in real estate, because he thinks he might have the knack of showing off houses and flats, Rod said he'd see what he could do in getting him an opening in a real estate brokerage firm that Vollard represents. Isn't that fine of Rod to take that much time out of his busy day to look after his poor brother-in-law?"

"Yes, it really is!" Jane exclaimed with sincere enthusiasm. She was always elated at any further proof of her husband's essential good will. And she knew that he would have gone carefully into the question of Bobby's capacity to handle such a new occupation and wouldn't land him in a job with which he couldn't cope. If anyone could get Bobby back on his feet, it would be Rod. And he would never say a word about it to anyone!

But there was another reason for Jane's welcoming of this evidence of her husband's humanity. For some time now she had been becoming concerned with the kind of law practice in which he so notoriously excelled. Was it as tough as some of her friends implied? Was it even brutal? When Rod was in the tense final moments of one of his corporate battles, when the chances of total victory or abysmal defeat seemed just about even, he would become silent and grim-featured, even at home, as if every corpuscle of his taut body and every nerve strand of his alert mind were arrayed for a last charge. At such times he would be distant; his evasive half-smile in answer to her questions hardly concealed his indifference to their purport; he barely noted what he ate or drank. Only in bed was he the same. Was it love or a kind of rape? Did he identify her body with the company he was trying to seize? Horrors!

She was embarrassed now when she recalled how she had quoted Byron to Harry Hammersly. It was one thing to be a corsair and put your life and that of your crew at a bold risk where only your strong right arm and flashing saber could assure their survival and conquest, but surely it was quite another to bury your opponents under mountains of writs and interrogatories, to ensnare them in the meshes of law, cleverly twisted, perhaps, to mean the very opposite of what their legislators intended. Jane had been brought up under the doctrine, placidly accepted by her parents and their world, that the so-called robber barons of the previous century were to be largely forgiven the legal corners they had cut in return for their having provided the nation with steel and oil and railroads. All very well — she had no quarrel with that — but what was the profit to our world today in Rod's internecine battles? Why wasn't he a corsair in the bad old sense of the word? And why wasn't Byron an ass to have idolized such a creature?

Rod's study was just off the library, and one night when he was working there and had left the door open, and she was seeking a book to read, she could hear him telephoning. When she heard him mention the name Meredith, she paused to listen. She knew it was the name of the president of the company his client was seeking to take over. It appeared that Mr. Meredith was to be offered a munificent sum.

She went to the doorway as he hung up. "What are you offering Mr. Meredith? A consolation prize?"

Rod was still so absorbed in his thoughts that he did not at once note the new tone in her voice.

"Meredith will have a good post in the amalgamated company," he replied.

"They've given in, then?"

"Not yet. But they will."

"You mean you're offering this man a fortune *before* he's given in? You're bribing him to betray his stockholders?"

Rod looked up at her with a sharpness that she had never felt before. Was she among the enemy now? And to be crushed?

"What has possessed you, Jane? There's no reason I shouldn't make plans on how to run the amalgamated companies. And I have no idea of dispensing with Joel Meredith's expertise. He can know it. You now can know it."

"But would you let the newspapers know it?"

"When I need you to advise me about my press relations, Jane, I'll let you know."

"But, Rod, don't you *see* what you're doing to that man? Don't you —"

He interrupted her firmly. "My dear, there are things about business you simply don't understand."

"And that I'm not supposed to ask about."

"You can ask all you like. And I'll be glad to explain the whole thing to you. I'm not doing anything, I promise you, that could get me into trouble, or of which you need feel in the least ashamed. Things are done differently today from the way they used to be done. That is all. But I have too much on my mind just now to go into it all. Forgive me, please, my dear. I have to make two more calls. I'll see you later."

"And I know how you'll buy my silence," she said bitterly and left the room.

But that night again he made love to her, and she was again the paramour of the corsair.

Resolving on the morrow that she would do well to smother her doubts about Rod's law practice, particularly as she could see she would never induce him to alter it, she decided to limit her interest in his firm to its social side. There was, it seemed, quite a bit of this: an annual outing for all in a country club, an annual dinner at Christmastime, semiannual partners' dinners, cocktail receptions for different office departments, and a tea for the lawyers' wives and the few women lawyers. As Mrs. Jessup she was invited to all of these, though Rod, who was inclined to downgrade such entertainments, assured her that she could pick and choose as she desired, or even attend none at all. But she now opted to be universal.

The other office wives were friendly but deferential. Most of the associates' wives and a goodly number of the younger partners' came from other parts of the country and had originally little social nucleus outside of the firm itself, so they had tended, at least in their first years, rather to cling together. They were also knit by the strong common denominator that held their mates: the obsession to get ahead in the firm. They all knew that Jane had a life and a fortune utterly independent of the firm, and they regarded her as a sort of bird of paradise who had oddly condescended to alight in their back yard, a phenomenon to be greeted with respect and even some awe, but not one to promote chumminess. Jane found herself really only at her ease with Vinnie, her husband's first wife, which the other women seemed to find faintly shocking. But Vinnie's background, after all, was closer to her own.

At the Vollard ladies' tea Jane allowed herself the independence of leading Vinnie to a corner for a twenty-minute private converse. Vinnie had no objection to this; since her father's stroke and the cessation of his active role in the firm, she had, despite Harry's prominence, taken little active part in these gatherings.

"Do you ever feel, Vinnie, as if the firm were standing between you and Harry?"

"A good many things stand between me and Harry," Vinnie replied, in a tone that implied that anything so well known need hardly be hid. "And I don't regard the firm as the most important of them. In some ways I wonder if it isn't the strongest bond between us. But you're thinking of Rod, of course. I quite see that the firm is something that Rod would not share with anyone, except with my father, and those days are long past. I even wonder sometimes how long he will share it with Harry."

This gave Jane a bit of a shock, but she decided that it was neither the time nor the place to go into it. "Did you ever find, when you and Rod were married, that there were sides of his nature that you didn't understand?"

This might have sounded a bit desperate, but Vinnie didn't seem in the least to mind. Her answer, however, was unexpected.

"Oh yes, there were, and I advise you to leave them strictly alone."

Jane discovered, however, on further questioning that that was all that Vinnie was going to yield, and her only available source for further information on the subject would have to be Harry. Harry, ever since her marriage to Rod, had insinuated flatteringly to her that she brought wit, culture and sympathy into both his legal and private lives, implying that these qualities had been sorely needed there. In society, where they often met, and even in office gatherings, he treated her with a gallantry whose exaggeration seemed to imply its innocence — or seemed to be intended to imply it. He would go so far as to interrupt a tête-à-tête that she might be holding with some gentleman at a party by demanding loudly, "Does your friend know about *us*, Jane?"

One day, when Harry was uptown in her neighborhood for the will-signing of a rich invalid client, he asked Jane to lunch with him at the Plaza, and she decided it would be the perfect occasion to quiz him about Rod and his law practice. She was well aware that Harry would delight in making things sound even worse than they were, but she thought she would know how to interpret this.

"I know people used to frown on these corporate raids, if that's what they're called," she began when they had finished their cocktails and were about to order. "But if everyone's doing them now, they can't be all that bad, can they?"

"Oh yes, they can!" Harry exclaimed cheerfully. "Face it, my dear, your husband and I are running a firm of shysters."

"Shysters! But Rod assures me that everything he does is strictly legal."

"Well, I should certainly hope so! That's what the clients pay him for. And through the nose, too. When I say we're shysters, I mean that's what we would have been called a generation back. Now the term has been cleaned up. In fact, it's rarely used anymore."

"What has changed it?"

"Prepare your pretty head for a little lecture. In the past, legal ethics required that an attorney should invoke the aid of a court only to recover a sum due, or for damages suffered by his client, or to prevent an anticipated wrong, or to enforce the performance of a legal duty. To sue in a court of law simply to harass a client's opponent into doing something he was not legally obliged to do would have been shysterism, pure and simple."

"And that is no longer the case?"

"Can you ask? Don't you read the newspapers? Nowadays, when one wishes to acquire a company that doesn't wish to be acquired, one's counsel bring all kinds of nuisance suits to induce it to change its mind. We sue for mismanagement by the directors, for unpaid dividends, for violation of the bylaws, for improper issuance of stock. We allege criminal misconduct; we shout about antitrust; we sue for ancient and dubious liabilities. And our opponent's counsel will answer with inordinate demands for all our files and seek endless interrogatories in order to enmesh our client in a hopeless tangle of red tape. But my point is that in no case is either party in the least interested in obtaining the objective for which it is ostensibly suing. It is simply war, and you know the quality that applies to that and love."

"And that's no longer being a shyster?"

"Only in the sense that everyone is. Oh yes, even the grandest of the grand old downtown firms. As they've moved to midtown, they've adjusted their standards. Even the 'most potent, grave and reverend signiors,' as Othello called them. Why not? It was the price of survival."

"And that's what Rod is so heroic about," she murmured. "Harassment."

"Well, there are all kinds of killers in the jungle, you know. There are some that play with their prey, like cats with mice, and some that start to eat them before they are dead, like hyenas, and some that kill for fun, like lions with cheetah cubs. But I'll say this for Rod. He's like the African wild dog, the swiftest and least painful killer who takes only just what he needs for his pack. Rod is the greatest artist at the game."

"But what does it all lead to?" Jane demanded with something like a wail. "Will companies keep swallowing companies until there are none left?"

"Or until only one is left!" Harry exclaimed with a delighted laugh. "One megacorporation making all the trash the world thinks it needs! And what will rise to put an end to this monster? What new Caligula, whose wish that humanity had but a single throat for him to cut has come true!"

"Oh, Harry, to you everything is a joke."

"I take *you* seriously enough, Jane dear."

She shrugged this off easily enough, but if she chose to ignore Harry's silly flirtiness, which to her was only his habit with pretty women, she was unable to prevent others from seeing implications in it. When she had to go down to the Vollard offices a few days later to consult one of the younger estate lawyers assigned by Rod to straighten out a tax wrinkle in her will, she ran into, of all people, Vinnie, who had been lunching with her father and who suddenly asked if she could have a few words with her.

"Here?" Jane asked, glancing dubiously around the impressively paneled reception hall hung with portraits of mostly dead partners. Ambrose Vollard, by a popular and expensive artist, clad unexpectedly in light tweeds and almost smiling, with eyes that seemed to wonder what you were doing there, loomed over the receptionist's desk.

"Why not?" Vinnie replied. "Though I suppose it's the last place in the world people would think I'd have chosen for what I have to say. Maybe that makes it the most appropriate."

"You intrigue me."

She followed Vinnie to a corner where they were relatively free from the clerks and office boys who crossed and recrossed the silent chamber.

"You lunched with Harry the other day," Vinnie began in a tone that seemed intent on not betraying an agitation that might have been expected but that she did not really feel. "At the Plaza. I don't think it's a good idea for you to be seen alone with him that way."

"You're afraid people might talk? I hope you don't think, Vinnie, that I have any idea of having an affair with your husband." Here she looked up at the portrait of Mr. Vollard. What had they all come to?

"I don't."

"Or he with me, for that matter."

"I don't think that either, Jane. Unless it happened to be part of a plan of his."

"What in God's name do you mean by that?"

"Harry's attitude towards Rod has always struck me as vaguely sinister. He professes to like and admire Rod, but I suspect that the underpinning of all that is envy. I think he envies Rod's looks and brains and the admiration he inspires. Don't you know what I mean, Jane? I think you do."

"I *do* see what you mean." Jane felt her shoulder twitch with a little shudder. "Like Iago and Cassio? 'He has a daily beauty in his life that makes me ugly.' Is that it? But what do you suppose he wants to do to Rod? *Tromper* him? With me? Make a cuckold of him?"

"He did it once before."

"*Did* he?" Jane looked sharply at Vinnie as she recalled what Harry had once told her. "But would it be like him to do the same thing twice? Isn't Harry more original than that. Besides, he's smart enough to know he'd never succeed with me."

"But he might make Rod think he had!"

"It *is* like *Othello*, then!" Jane exclaimed, almost excited by the idea. "The business of making your victim believe your lie." But her thrill over the literary analogy had a quick death. "But that isn't his game either, is it?" Her spirits sank as she beheld the ashy truth. "It's something worse. He wants to take the beauty, as he sees it, out of Rod's life. He wants to make him as ugly as he is. He wants Rod to be just the kind of lawyer he is. Oh, how I see it now!"

"But Harry considers himself a great lawyer!" Vinnie protested.

"Rod doesn't consider him that. And Harry knows only too well that Rod doesn't." Jane rose now. She had learned everything she had to learn. "I must go, Vinnie. But don't worry. I shan't forget your warning. No more lunches at the Plaza."

There had been a kind of tacit agreement between Jane and her husband that they would embark on no further discussions of his specialty in law, but that night she broke it. She also broke her resolution never to intrude again on his study when he was working late. She strode into it now and boldly took a seat before his desk.

"Well!" he exclaimed, looking up in surprise. "Something must have happened to put that grim look on your lovely features."

"Something has. Vinnie thinks I shouldn't be seen lunching with Harry."

"Are you?"

"We lunched together at the Plaza last week."

"Did you?"

"You don't sound upset."

"Should I be?"

"No. I just wanted to see if you would be. And it's not really what I came in here to discuss. I want you to know just how Harry describes your business."

She watched him carefully as she carefully attempted to paraphrase everything that Harry had told her. He said nothing. But his face slowly congealed into a hardness that almost frightened her. When she had finished, he still said nothing.

"I feel like Elsa in the opera," she stammered nervously. "Have I asked Lohengrin to tell me his name?" She made a poor effort to laugh. "Will you call for a swan?"

For answer he simply stacked the papers before him in a neat pile and put them to one side. "Thanks for telling me, Jane. I guess it's time we went to bed."

But that night he didn't make love to her. She even wondered if he might not be jealous. She almost hoped so. Jealousy was something with which she thought she could cope.

13

ROD SAT IN HIS OFFICE the next morning, his door un-
characteristically closed, his secretary instructed that he would
take no calls, unable or at least unwilling to face any part of the
work suggested by the pile of memoranda prepared by his
faithful and industrious clerks. It was as if the foggy bank of
sleaze that had invaded every cubbyhole of his existence, and
which his vainly shut portal could hardly keep away from his
nostrils, had now soiled the last vestiges of his valiant efforts
to achieve a new and freer life. Harry Hammersly was everywhere. He had taken Rod's wife, his daughters, his father-in-
law; he had not only made over Rod's firm in his own hateful
image, he had made Rod an integral part of the whole jerry-
built new structure. And finally, by the most ironical of twists,
he had married Rod to the beautiful, wonderful and adorable
Jane. Oh yes, Jane was all those things and more, but she was
still a gift from Harry. And her world was Harry's world, even
when, as an essentially helpless woman, she had bravely condemned it.

He did not see how he could go on in that world. He certainly no longer wanted to. The picture that Jane had so vividly
sketched for him, of Harry laughing and sneering at the very
kind of law that he had acquired Rod to practice on a greater

scale, seemed to show Harry as equating Rod with himself and himself with Rod, as if he were gleefully offering two damned souls to his devil of a boss who had at last overthrown God. It had to be the last version in the epic of Rod's self-delusion.

But maybe he could simply walk away from it all, resign his partnership and flee to some desert like an anchorite of old. Maybe he could escape, clutching some poor remnant of what he had liked to consider his old dignity. Would Jane go with him? Would she even renounce her fortune, as smacking of Harry's hell? Rod rubbed his eyes as he recognized the madness of such an idea. But *was* he mad? Not yet. He still knew that there was no "work of noble note" yet to be done "not unbecoming men that strove with gods." But if one let go the "noble note," mightn't there be a work, however less than noble, to leave at least a parting glow on Götterdämmerung?

And then his mind seemed to erupt into a tawny blast. There had to be a way, and perhaps there *was* a way, to kick Harry back into the dark abyss from which he had crawled! Was it madness or inspiration that put him suddenly in mind of old Mr. Tilley and his muttered hints.

Mr. Tilley, or "Tilley," as he was generally known in the office, even by messenger boys fifty years his junior (did he even have a first name?), was the longtime bursar and head of the accounting department; he seemed like an old servant of the Bourbons surviving faithfully but shaggily into the glaring and bewildering sunshine of Napoleonic life. But he was still accomplished at his trade, and he continued to hold his sway over a department of some half-dozen others, more than one of whom had had to recognize his inability to replace him. Tilley was in charge of keeping the books of all the estates and trusts of which Harry Hammersly was a fiduciary.

The old man's relationship with Rod was based on his devotion to the now inactive Ambrose Vollard and his treasured memory of how close Rod had been to the former managing partner. Tilley made little effort to hide his low opinion of the Hammersly regime — no open censure escaped his lips, but his puckered brow or shrug were plain enough — and though it must have troubled him to see Rod so closely associated with the new power, he seemed still to harbor the stubborn faith that the once bright knight of Mr. Vollard might yet be on the side of the angels.

As Rod had little to do with trusts and estates, Tilley had few opportunities to consult with him, but after Rod's marriage and the handing over to the firm's accountants some of Jane's financial matters, he had the occasion at times to intrude upon Rod's busy schedule in quest of certain decisions. Rod always took the time out after their business was concluded to ask about the old man's bachelor life, his dog and his cat and his passion for the Yankees. Tilley always lingered for a moment in the doorway before departing, as if there was something on his mind that he wasn't sure would be gratefully received.

"What is it, Tilley?" Rod had felt called upon to ask one day. "Is there something else on your mind?"

"Well, I was just wondering, sir . . ." Tilley now stepped timidly back into Rod's office. "I was just wondering if you mightn't take a little more interest in our trust accountings. You have such a natural flair for figures, sir, as I can see in the way you handle your wife's affairs."

"It's nice of you to say that, Tilley. But my wife's matters are enough for me. I can leave all the rest to Mr. Hammersly, can't I? That department is really his, isn't it?"

"Oh yes, it is, sir! And he's the fiduciary of some of our biggest trusts. Quite a little empire he has there, sir. Quite a little empire."

"And I suppose he's a benevolent despot?"

"A despot, sir?" Tilley's laugh was a dry cackle. "That's a good one. Yes, sir, that's a good one."

"I said a benevolent despot, Tilley."

"Oh yes, sir, benevolent." Again that laugh. "That's even better."

Rod had now frowned. "Tilley, are you trying to tell me something about Mr. Hammersly's trusts?"

The poor man paled at his tone. "No sir. I guess not, sir." And he fled.

Rod had not thought of this again, but now it lit up his whole mind. He picked up his telephone and summoned the bursar to his office. When the old man appeared, Rod closed the door behind him and stood like a prosecuting attorney, his back to the window.

"I want you, Tilley, to tell me all you know about Mr. Hammersly's performance as a trustee. I'll be perfectly frank with you. I have an idea that you know things I ought to know."

"Things?" Tilley looked almost sly.

"Maybe even bad things. Whatever they are, you have my word that I'll back you up and protect you against anyone who objects to your having spoken to me. Is that fair? Don't you think I ought to know, Tilley? Wouldn't Mr. Vollard have wanted to know?"

"Oh, he would, sir!"

"Then take a seat and relax and tell me all."

Tilley needed no further encouragement. Seated stiffly and facing his interlocutor he made what was probably the longest speech of his lifetime. Rod did not once interrupt him.

"Well, sir, you know Mr. Hammersly has a way with the ladies. Particularly old ladies. And particularly, I should add, wealthy old ladies. And if they happen to be a bit weak in the upper story, he has even more of a way. Take Mrs. Elkins, for example. She has been judicially declared incompetent and has only one child, a daughter who lives in Paris and is never heard from so long as she receives her huge monthly check from the guardian of Mama's property who is, of course, your noted partner. But it was Mrs. Elkins's habit, when she was possessed of what we politely referred to as her sound mind, to donate large annual sums to charities, some of which, highly dubious, were known for their flattering ways. Mr. Hammersly decided to change all that. He obtained an order from the surrogate allowing him to continue the incompetent's former generosity, but instead of the dubious charities he substituted the highly reputable ones of the Andrews Settlement House and World Missions. Very fine, wasn't it? Only the House and the Missions happened to have as their chairman one Harry Hammersly and as their counsel his firm. They added to the luster of his public image and to his client-attractive reputation. And that, sir, is indeed the motive behind every action Mr. Hammersly takes as fiduciary. In his other trusts he invested heavily in capital ventures of considerable risk and ones in which he, too, was personally involved. As executor of the Lamb estate he took it upon himself to forgive the outstanding notes of the Lincolnville Country Club of which he is president, and in settling the suit of the Clyde Baker trust against a patently fraudulent and easily defeated plaintiff, he charged the huge fee of . . ."

And so it went, on and on. When Tilley had at last finished his diatribe, Rod grimly made him repeat it all, this time taking careful notes and making sharp inquiries.

He gave himself overnight to study these revelations, and early the next morning he marched down the long corridor to Harry's office and took a threatening stance before the latter's desk. Harry was purring into the telephone, presumably to one of his rich female clients.

"But, sweetie, there's no law that requires you to give all that nice stock to your children. Which of your daughters asked you to? Was it Goneril or Regan? Yes, of course they're from *King Lear*. A tragedy every parent ought to read, mark and inwardly digest. Now don't give me figures. I know all the figures; that's my trade. And I can also tell you, at no extra charge, that if you spend all your money on yourself, there won't be any estate tax, either. Oh, of course, I don't mean that literally. I agree you should do something for the little darlings, if that's what they really are. All I'm telling you, my dear, is that you should look after yours truly first and foremost. After you have decided that you really have enough to ensure your complete comfort for what we trust will be a very protracted lifetime, then we'll see what we can do for your posterity. And now, love, I must ring off, as my partner Rod Jessup — you remember handsome Rod, don't you? Oh yes, I *thought* you would — is glaring at me as if he were going to break our luncheon engagement. Who will share my noontime martini? Goodbye!" He hung up and winked at Rod. "The one sure way to gain the love of the rich, my boy, is to tell them they're not spending enough money on themselves."

Rod turned abruptly to Harry's secretary, who appeared in the doorway as he finished his call. "Please leave us alone, Miss Peltz, close the door and don't put through any calls while I'm here."

"You can't do that, Rod!" Harry exclaimed. "I'm expecting a call from Nicky at Morgan Stanley."

"He can wait."

Harry reluctantly nodded to his secretary to do as Rod told her, and they were left alone.

"It had better be important, Rod."

"It *is* important."

Rod, still standing, recited the table that he had learned by heart, in short, brusque, matter-of-fact sentences. Harry did not once interrupt, though he did gaze twice out the window, as if he were faintly bored. Was it possible that he wasn't even very much surprised?

"You haven't dug up anything really new, Rodman," he said at last. "One of our younger partners, who assists me with the trusts, has given me the same spiel. I know there are risks in the way I operate, but they are risks that I've carefully assessed. One thing — and I believe it's the essence of the matter — of which you don't seem in the least conscious, is that every so-called venturesome investment that I have made for my trusts has resulted in substantial gains for them. You haven't heard any beneficiaries complain, have you? Damn right, you haven't! And the fact that I had some of my own funds in every venture was helpful. As a partner in each deal I had ways to find out what was really going on, which lessened the risk. And in the Elkins matter I substituted reputable charities for the rickety ones the poor old lady had been duped into supporting. As for the Lamb deal, that country club was damn near bust and could never have paid the notes, besides which Lamb had told me in his lifetime that the transaction was meant to be a gift. The other matters I could take up one by one —"

Rod interrupted. "But the point is that the primary beneficiary in each case was yourself."

"Helping oneself can often be the surest way of helping others."

"That certainly seems to have been your guiding principle. How do you think the surrogate would react if he heard it?"

"Very badly, I admit. But would I be surcharged? What would be the damages?"

"Nothing would be lost, as Jim Fisk put it, but honor. And you might be asked to resign your fiduciary positions. Which I'll save the courts the trouble of doing by asking it of you now."

"You're asking me to give up my trusts? Have you taken leave of your senses?"

"Very likely."

"What would that do to the firm?"

"It might hurt for a while. But we'd survive. And in the long run we'd all be the better for it."

"I have to assume you're serious. Of course, I refuse."

"You'll fight me on this? With what you know I can show the partners?"

"To the last ditch. Somebody may get kicked out, but are you so damn sure it will be me?" Harry now moderated his tone. "Look, Rod. You're sick. You need to see a doctor. Don't do this to the firm. Talk to Jane."

"What's Jane got to do with it?"

"She makes sense, anyway. Do you mind if I talk to her?"

"I don't care who you talk to."

Which Harry did, that very afternoon, for when Rod got home she was waiting for him tensely in the living room. She rose and tried to put her arms around him, but he held her off.

"Darling, I don't care what Harry's done — you can't do this to him. You can't destroy the firm you and he have built."

"*He* and I!"

"Well, haven't you? And is what you've been doing so very different from what he has?"

Rod stared at her. "You mean we both should be disbarred? Maybe you're right at that!"

"Oh, Rod, if that were the real reason you were going after him, perhaps I wouldn't so much mind. But it isn't! It's something black and horrid deep down inside you that you've got to be rid of!"

"What is it, in God's name?"

"I don't know! But if you do this thing, I'll . . . I'll leave you, that's all!"

And she ran from the room in a fit of tears.

Rod felt a crashing in his ears. He had a sudden searing vision of Samson pulling down the temple on himself.

14

HETTY SHATTUCK, AS SHE WAS, forty years back, before she married Ambrose Vollard, suffered as a child severe attacks of asthma, from which her ultimate recovery was almost complete, but which for several years darkened her life with terrible gasping fits of breathlessness. Her keenest and most enduring memories of this painful period were of her benign and caring father taking hours out of his busy clergyman's day simply to sit silently by her bed and radiate sympathy and love from every pore of his large and richly clad clerical body. He would also, when she was feeling well enough to listen, endeavor to comfort her with some of the precepts of his faith, assuring her that her courage in bearing her discomforts was appreciated by a deity who had suffered himself all the pains that human flesh could endure. Her mother was less articulate on this subject. As a good Boston spouse Naomi Shattuck left all matters of religion wisely and conclusively in the hands of a husband so uniquely qualified to handle them, but she offered equal comfort to her afflicted daughter. And Hetty, regarding them with the detachment of an invalid resigned to her fate, was able to love them as well as assess them.

She saw them as souls favored by fortune, born to health, prosperity and riches and even more blessed by having the talent to relish and enjoy their benefits. They believed implicitly in a god who had showered these boons upon them, requiring only in return that they should lead virtuous existences, which they were only too happy to do. That she, Hetty, had been born under a different star with different liabilities, did not strike her as unjust or even cruel; it was simply the way things were. And she was somewhat compensated by being freed of the restricting religious views that had illuminated or clouded, depending on the point of view, the skies of her parents and her forebears and of the founders of the Massachusetts Bay Colony themselves. But as she made it out, in her own careful and reflective way, this freedom applied only to thought and not to actions. Her activities, she was somehow sure, had to be as circumspect as those of all the other Shattucks. She was fated to be a true New Englander, after all.

What it seemed to boil down to was that if she was a good girl, the world would be nice to her. And she liked having the world nice to her, particularly when the world was made up of persons as dear as Mummy and Daddy and her brothers and sisters. Nor was it very hard, after all, to be a good girl.

And when she regained her health it was even easier. Hetty grew up to live at peace with a universe that, like Margaret Fuller, she had learned to accept. But that she was the acutest observer in her family was no secret to her parents and siblings; they cheerfully accused her of hidden heresies. Boston had no hostility to heresies that were veiled; Boston cared only for form, for propriety. Boston — and Hetty welcomed it as her salvation — didn't care what you thought or even very much what you said so long as your outward demeanor conformed to the accepted norm. Boston was wise, even perhaps civilized.

The historian Brooks Adams, a cousin of her mother's (all of old Boston was kin), was a case in point. His dress, his demeanor and his conduct conformed perfectly to the social code; his ancestry was historic and his social circle select, so nobody objected to his scathing denunciations of the early fathers of the commonwealth or to his stark reports of their religious bigotry and savage persecutions. Even at the Reverend Philemon Shattuck's board he was a constantly welcomed guest, and young Hetty, whose independence of mind he soon discovered, became almost his confidante. Adams, with the egocentricity of an obsessed and aristocratic scholar, made little distinction between those who had the patience to hear him sound off; a young girl and an old man were the same to him if he felt a response. To Hetty he became an oracle, the one human being who saw the world not necessarily as it was — for what was that? — but as she saw it.

That her forebears should have fled religious intolerance in the old world to establish it in the new seemed no odder to her than that she should enjoy her father's beautiful garden in summers in Nahant while the poor sweltered in the city slums. The symphony of different shades of green bushes and trees that she viewed from a cool terrace was all that man could do with the disorder of nature, and she applauded the victory, however brief, however doomed, of art over weeds. Her particular passion was history, and in history her greatest love was Gibbon, whose massive volumes of Roman history she read and reread, finding in them, more than anywhere else, the true picture of the human condition. The rise and fall of kingdoms and empires, attended by the same ambitions and the same decays, the endless repetition of devastating wars and massacres, the tinselly splendor and the gruesome gore, the old gods and the new, the theological superstitions and the religious hatreds — how could anyone endowed with her vision see a design in it? How could she see anything but chaos interrupted by monotony?

Yet Gibbon, it was finally revealed to her, did make something out of it. He extracted a history out of it, and his history, like her father's garden, was a work of art. That was the one answer that man could cast in the grinning face of pointlessness; those long golden sentences were coiled around the fleeting annals of the decline and fall of the western and eastern empires. Hetty had no reason to suppose that she herself would have the escape of becoming a writer; she was willing to content herself with the role of observer. But of an observer from whom nothing is concealed.

In Ambrose Vollard the now maturer Hetty professed to see a kind of latter-day Germanicus or Marcellus, one of those noble Roman heroes on whom history seems to shine a brief spotlight, spread a wild hope in the surrounding shadows, soon quelled, that a day of redemption may be actually at hand and that a firm administration is at last going to check the barbarians and restore dignity and rule to the Roman state. Such interludes, anyway, are gratifying to the watcher, and Hetty was determined to be that. What she had not counted on was that she should fall, for the first and last time in her life, violently in love.

She was fated to take her crystal vision with her to New York and to her married life in that metropolis. It was not long before she could see that if Germanicus had ideals — and Ambrose certainly did — he was going to insist that those ideals be shared by all. If he had the stout heart of Marcellus, he had also the egotism of Augustus. This, however, could have been acceptable to a handmaiden of Gibbon had she occupied in her husband's affections the position that she had once almost dared hope she might. And, of course, she had not. He was a man's man who, however much he might refuse to acknowledge it, even perhaps to himself, could never regard a woman as a true soul mate. A wife was a kind of junior partner in the law firm of his life, maybe even a senior associate, and a daughter, like Vinnie, a sort of playful kitten until she had grown into a cat. Neither Hetty nor her eldest daughter could ever take over the role that Rod had played in Ambrose's life nor hope to fill the gap that he had left.

All this should have been foreseeable to a Boston virgin of supposedly Emersonian tranquillity, and to some extent it had been, but if Hetty had miscalculated the stubborn masculinity of her husband's nature, she had also underestimated the jealous femininity of her own. She discovered to her dismay that she was unable to accept with a philosophical equanimity her cameo role in the Vollard order of things, and that she was more and more giving voice to little jabs of biting humor that gave her the local reputation of a brilliant wit but that led often to a rather sullen silence at the family board.

Since Ambrose's stroke, however, these tensions had greatly eased. His condition had now become pitiable, smothering her least resentments. Hetty knew herself to be a wonderful nurse. She always managed to be where she was needed, without ever seeming to hover. Her agile mind anticipated her patient's every need, without his having either pathetically or petulantly to ask, and her anecdotes of the world outside the sickroom were always fresh and amusing. Ambrose, who understood perfectly just how and why she was transforming herself, did her the honor of never thanking her. He knew he now had a treasure, and a treasure too proud to be told what it was.

When he got better and returned to his office, where he was of little use except to sign documents in matters of which he was still a fiduciary, she knew that he would waste some of his partners' time by dropping into their offices to chat of old times, but she also knew how important this diversion was to him, and she used all of her still considerable influence in the firm to see that it was tolerated. She worked particularly on Harry Hammersly, who was somewhat in awe of his mother-in-law and kept a wary eye on her ample portfolio of market securities.

"If things get too bad, come to me," she warned him. "And I'll speak to Ambrose. But not till then. You mustn't let any of your partners forget how much they owe him."

"Some of the younger ones are hardly aware of that, Mrs. V."

Rod had been allowed to call her Hetty; Harry never.

"Then you must instruct them," she said grimly.

"Aye aye, ma'am."

One day, when she had gone downtown to Ambrose's office to sign a codicil adding a bequest to the newly born child of her youngest daughter, her husband had asked her to stay on afterwards to hear something which, as soon as the witnesses to the codicil had left, he wanted to impart to her.

It was about the row between Rod and Harry. Harry had been in his father-in-law's office the first thing that morning to beg him to try to pound some sense into Rod's hot head.

Hetty shook her head ruefully as she took in the details of the quarrel. She had long anticipated a blowout between her present and ex sons-in-law. The barbarians were at the gates of Rome as the consuls bickered. She took quick note, however, of one essential fact.

"But if there have been no losses in the trusts," she pointed out, "why can't Harry put them back in order? Sell the wrong things and buy the right ones? And agree to stop favoring his pet charities?"

"He could do those things, of course. And he's even agreed to do them. But Rod wants blood! He wants Harry to resign all his fiduciary positions. He claims he's not fit to hold them!"

"And there may be something in what he says. But surely if he keeps an eye on Harry in the future, that will stop him from these excesses. After all, Harry is supposed to be a first-class fiduciary. Everyone seems to want him."

"But Rod's inexorable. And do you know something, Hetty? In a way I can't blame him."

"But, Ambrose, this thing may split your firm wide open!"

"And maybe it's about time for that. We used to represent a kind of high-water mark among the great firms. And now, under the joint leadership of our eldest daughter's two husbands we have become what? Another wolf pack. Let it blow itself up, I say. It should make a splendid bonfire!"

"For you to enjoy watching. Shame on you, Ambrose. I never heard anything so selfish. Maybe I'd better speak to Rod myself."

"Stay out of it, Hetty. It's no longer really your or my affair."

"And it wouldn't do any good, either, I suppose. When Rod gets his teeth into something there's no letting go."

"You and I belong to the past, my dear. And I like to think a glorious one. Even if that's only fancy. Shall I take you out for a very good lunch?"

But she knew how much he craved the table reserved daily for any Vollard partners who cared to join it at his lunch club and firmly took her departure.

In the reception hall a man hurried after her and caught her by the elbow. It was a very distraught-looking Rod.

"Hetty, where are you going?"

"Home, dear boy."

"Not till you've lunched with me!"

"Rod, I'm sorry. I can't."

"Please!"

"No!"

"For God's sake, Hetty!"

To her horror he dropped to his knees. Right there, in the august reception area, before the astonished girl at the main desk and the gaping office boys.

"Rod, get up! All right. Let's get out of here!"

He jumped to his feet and guided her to the elevator. After a five-minute walk, in which a severe silence was maintained, they faced each other over a booth table in the nearest restaurant.

"I'm sure Ambrose has told you our problem," he began.

"He has told me *your* problem."

"You don't see it as ours? As yours and mine? As the firm's?"

"Well, I see it as more particularly yours. Because you're making it so. Perhaps because you even want to make it so."

"You sound like Jane." Rod's eyes seemed desperately to plead his cause. "She's even threatening to leave me!"

"Do you want her to?"

"Oh, Hetty! How can you say that? You, of all people."

"Because, as I see it, everything is entirely in your control. If you don't put things back in order, it must be because you wish the mess to remain."

"Oh, you mean let Harry fix it all up."

"Just so."

"Or cover it all up. Abet a crime, is that it?"

"Not at all. Rectify an error."

"Which he may repeat at will in the future?"

"He won't. Don't worry. He may lack scruples but he's no fool. Besides, you'll have old Tilley to keep an eye on him. You can live with Harry, Rod. We all have."

"And with the kind of firm he's turned Ambrose's old one into?"

"You have so far. And is it really so different from what it was?"

"Oh, Hetty!" he exclaimed again.

"You forget, my dear, that I grew up in a time when insider trading was a coveted privilege and not a crime. When the maneuvering of stock prices for the benefit of a favored few was considered good business and not a fraud on the public. And where monopoly was God and the Morgan partners his apostles. I learned that morals change with the weather. You may not like Harry, but at least he knows how to find happiness."

"Spare me his way!"

"It has indeed been spared you, poor boy. You are a genius at cultivating your own misfortune." She reached a hand over to pat his. "Don't lose Jane, whatever you do."

Tears sprang up in his eyes. "Hetty, what's wrong with me?"

"Well, perhaps I should start by telling you that I always knew why you started that business with Mrs. Fisk. You knew all about Vinnie and Harry, didn't you?"

"How in God's name did you know that?"

"It was the only thing that made it all add up."

"And did you tell them? Did you tell Ambrose?"

"I didn't tell a soul. I didn't see it was any of their business. They had their own principles or life styles or whatever you want to call it. They could work it out for themselves."

"And have they? Vinnie and Harry?"

"I think so. In their own way. Vinnie finally faced — what she must have always suspected — that she had been thoroughly used. Now she's much less subservient. She knows that if Harry doesn't give her everything she wants, she can do him a lot of damage. And Harry knows that. As I say, he's no fool. Besides, he still has something of a physical hold over Vinnie. She's a passionate woman, that child of mine, and she hasn't got any prettier with increased avoirdupois. If she had to get another man today, she'd have to buy one."

Rod looked as shocked as he undoubtedly was. "I take it you're not much drawn to your son-in-law."

"Drawn to him? I detest him."

"Is he aware of that?"

"Oh, he misses nothing. But he's not afraid I'll do anything to harm him. He's smart enough to know that people like me, who have no reserves in their thinking, are the opposite in their acting. They don't care to rock boats. Perhaps because truth is enough for them without always seeking to establish it. Or is it because they see how often action is futile? If they know that thought at all, they also know how little it's worth."

"So if everything's pretty much the same today as it was yesterday the only difference is that now there may be less hypocrisy?"

"There's certainly less of it. Indeed, I wonder at times if there's any of it left. And I must admit I miss it. Justice Holmes said once that the sight of heroism bred a faith in heroism. And I don't see much heroism in the world about me."

"Are you losing your faith in it? Harry used to proclaim that he believed in no absolute moral rules. That there was only taste, and that good taste was what kept people from sordid crimes like murder and robbery."

"I had the good taste, anyway, to see little good in Harry. And I prefer the old Rod Jessup to the new."

"And what was the old Rod Jessup?"

"A proud, stiff, idealistic puritan right out of the pages of Nathaniel Hawthorne!"

"And an anachronism."

"But such a pretty one. Leave me to my memories. They're all I've got." And she turned to the menu.

"Let's have a drink first, Hetty. To some kind of synthesis between the old and the new Rod. I'll make it up with Harry. And of course I'll call Jane." He signaled to a waiter. "And there's something else. Something that came over me last night when I was debating what I'd do with myself if the firm really broke up. I decided that if I went on with the takeover business I'd only represent defendants! How does that strike you as a move forward in legal ethics?"

Hetty decided not to reply to this until their cocktails arrived, and after she had drunk hers, not to reply at all except in a gracious affirmative. She had learned enough about his practice to know that the defense used just as many dirty tricks as the offense, but she was warned by something (a good angel appearing in her customarily unwelcoming sky?) to hold her tongue. She was in the healthful process of saving her beloved ex-son-in-law, and she could hardly expect to take more than one or two steps at a time. As it was, she had averted Armageddon.